# THE BOYFRIEND
# MATERIAL NOVELLAS

## LAUREN BLAKELY

# ABOUT THE BOYFRIEND MATERIAL NOVELLAS

Now available in one set for the first time, you can enjoy the two novellas in the Boyfriend Material series and indulge in these sexy, feel-good romantic comedies!

## Special Delivery

All I want for the holidays is the secret potion that'll help me resist my brother's new business partner. You know, the super hot, super sweet, super smart guy I now have to plan the holiday party with.

I mean, really. Who thought THAT was a good idea?

Oh, me. Yep, brilliant, strategic me who raised her hand and said yes I'd love to hang mistletoe with that sexy former sports star. I'd love to taste test spiked hot chocolate with that charming, flirty man. I'd love to get snowed in with the one guy I shouldn't fall for.

As long as I can make it through the holidays I'll be on my merry way, fa la la la la. But the holidays have a surprise for me.

### Your French Kisses

To do list for my last day of my Paris vacation...
1. Walk along the river
2. Visit all the chocolate shops in the city
3. Wander along the cobblestone streets.

Things I don't expect to happen...

1. Meet a charming Englishman while strolling along the Seine
2. Spend the afternoon with him exploring Paris, and kissing. So many French kisses...
3. Board a plane that night wishing I'd gotten his last name.

Besides, you can't fall for someone in one day, especially when you live a world apart...

# SPECIAL DELIVERY

# ABOUT

All I want for Christmas is the secret potion that'll help me resist my brother's new business partner. You know, the super hot, super sweet, super smart guy I now have to plan the holiday party with.

I mean, really. Who thought THAT was a good idea?

Oh, me. Yep, brilliant, strategic me who raised her hand and said yes I'd love to hang mistletoe with that sexy former sports star. I'd love to taste test spiked hot chocolate with that charming, flirty man. I'd love to get snowed in with the one guy I shouldn't fall for.

As long as I can make it through the holidays I'll be on my merry way, fa la la la la. But the holidays have a surprise for me.

# SPECIAL DELIVERY

By Lauren Blakely

Want to be the first to learn of sales, new releases, preorders and special freebies? Sign up for my VIP mailing list here!

# HIS PROLOGUE

*Vaughn*

When I started my new business, I made three pledges.

First: always kick ass for my clients.

Second: leave the past far behind.

Third: run like hell from entanglements of the *romantic kind.*

I don't just mean taboo trysts with clients or coworkers. My rule has always been to avoid those like a communal bowl of pretzels at a bar.

A communal *anything anywhere,* for that matter.

When I say "entanglements," I mean of any sort with any woman to any degree—whether that is love, sex, or dating.

Yeah, the whole shebang, *bang* and all.

I'm no good at balance anyway. I'm an all-or-nothing kind of guy, and I need to give my all to my new gig.

So the other side gets nada.

I don't discriminate in my sidestep-women-at-all-costs strategy—clients, coworkers, and business partners are off-limits, and so are their sisters, cousins, and any other female relatives. The "nothing" side means no women from Match, Tinder, or any dating app; no women friends, friends of friends, or friends of my sisters who they would love to set me up with; no women I meet in my building or my gym or on my route to work, not even that cute woman who arranges flowers at the shop where I order a bouquet delivered to my mom in Florida every Sunday.

Maybe it sounds hard to go cold turkey—or, let's be honest, more like full-on frozen turkey.

But romance isn't that difficult to dodge if you have a strategy.

And I don't mean a playboy plan; that dip-the-wick-daily lifestyle never interested me.

I think of it like a diet, and I damn well need it if I'm going to be in fighting shape for work. The last time I fell hard for someone, I spent the better part of a year cleaning up the mess that it made of my work life. I have no desire to venture down that path again.

That means no cheat days. No sneaking into the pantry for a kiss with a sexy lady here or snagging a tasty-looking cookie from the one-night-stand jar of treats.

Fine, sometimes dessert seduces me, and I've always been a sucker for sweets. But as a former pro athlete, I have excellent discipline, and I'm feeling pretty cocky about my ability to resist temptation.

At least, I *had been*. Then I met someone who makes me want to devour her—à la mode with a layer of hot fudge.

Only, I suspect Quinn would be sweet on her own.

Sexy, clever, witty, captivating Quinn.

Since I met her, I want every day to be a break from my diet. I want to indulge my sweet tooth at breakfast, lunch, and dinner.

It won't be easy, but the solution is obvious. I need to go on a *Quinn fast*. I'll simply abstain from seeing her.

*Ever again.*

Then I find out we'll be working side by side through the holidays.

Deck the halls with my greatest temptation, and fuck me sideways with a nutcracker.

Fa-la-la-la-la.

# HER PROLOGUE

*Quinn*

Spoiler alert—I love spoilers.

I adore them like they're a new pair of sexy, stylish shoes that fit like they're made for me.

Less of a surprise—I hate surprises.

My sisters know to never throw me a surprise party, and my brother is on notice—no uninvited pop-in visits to my apartment. *Or else.*

Because I know all their childhood secrets and I'm not afraid to use them.

But as long as my sibs comply, I *won't* let slip when exactly my brother stopped running around the house naked (he was six), or how many posters of Mr. Darcy my little sister pinned to her walls (more than ten).

Or maybe I wouldn't. I'm not *evil.*

I simply can't stand the suspense of not knowing what's going to happen.

Like how I googled the ending of the most recent *Avengers* movie. I don't even watch Marvel flicks, but I was dying to know why my social media feed was suddenly full of shocked reaction gifs. (And I've got to say—holy smokes—I didn't see *that* coming.)

Why *wouldn't* I read the endings of books first? I wasn't going to devote all that time to Matthew and Elizabeth in *A Discovery of Witches* otherwise. And settling in on a Friday night with *Memento* on Netflix, my popcorn tasted so much better after I checked the plot summary for a road map to that twisty-as-a-DNA-strand flick.

When it comes to holidays—well, it will shock no one to learn that I was the kid who opened her Christmas presents in advance.

*Sorry, Mom and Dad.*

I crept out of bed in the wee hours of the morning, tiptoed downstairs, and slid my finger under the wrapping paper to peek inside.

So, yes, that puts me on the naughty list. But I learned to wrap presents like a Macy's gift-wrapping counter pro and impress my friends. Show me a champion gift wrapper, and I'll show you a former present-peeker.

I need to know what's around the corner and five steps ahead. Given my aversion to suspense, I'd make a terrible adventurer, ghost hunter, or cop.

But I make an excellent event planner.

Planning is my jam, and organizing feeds my soul.

Even better, I love celebrations, people, and good conversations that last long into the night.

It's the perfect job for me, keeping me sane, and lately it's been the perfect medicine. After my last relationship went up less in flames and more in an epic bonfire of pain and sadness, my business—Quinn Summers Events—was a salve.

I refuse to let my heart be blindsided again, which means steering clear of love and men for a long time to come.

That's a cinch for a spoiler-loving gal like me. All it takes to avoid love and romance is a little forward thinking. For instance, when my brother asks me to work with his business partner to plan a series of holiday parties for his new firm, I do what I do best.

*I peek.*

I have to know what's in the box, so I lift the curtain and google his business partner, a certain Vaughn Channing, former Super Bowl-winning tight end for the San Francisco Renegades.

*Oh me. Oh my. Hello, handsome.*

Just look at him there in his football uniform, catching a touchdown pass.

And wow. Check him out these days in the tailored suit he wears as a dealmaker. Why, yes, the former pro-baller-turned-sports-agent is just my type.

Well, I do like men who are handsome as hell, fit as fiddles, and smile like they're legitimately happy.

He ticks all three boxes.

This is why it's good to know what's around the bend. Now I'm prepped for peak resistance when I head to dinner to meet him for the first time.

I'm armed with mantras and positive affirmations.

*Don't flirt. Do resist. You are the consummate professional.*

Except spoiler alert—*I cave.*

Oh hell, do I ever cave, and fast.

But our ending is one I never saw coming.

# 1

## VAUGHN

My calendar says it's a week after Halloween, but tell that to Manhattan.

The city has draped itself in red, green, and candy cane. Fake icicles frost the streetlamps, paper snowflakes flurry in store windows, and blue-and-white strings of lights flicker from building balconies.

As I walk past a Duane Reade display peddling Santa toilet paper—*Seriously? Santa deserves way better*—I snap a picture and shoot it over to my sister Callie while we chat on the phone.

"New York is a freaking winter wonderland already. How is this possible?" I ask. "I gave out Halloween candy last week, and now it's jingle all the way."

"Where did you give out candy? In your penthouse apartment?"

"It's not the penthouse, and it won't be mine much longer," I point out as I turn onto Madison Avenue, heading toward the offices of Premiere Agency where I work.

"Last time I saw your place, it was pretty damn swank." She sounds like she's caught me in a fib—such an attorney.

"But it's not the penthouse. I live on the tenth floor. The building has eleven floors, counselor."

"A technicality," she deadpans. "I'll rephrase my statement: you don't live in a penthouse on Park Avenue—you're slumming it a story below in a tenth-floor two-bedroom. You're sooo ordinary."

"See? I'm just like everyone else."

She laughs, and I know she's rolling her eyes. "Right. Except for the three years you played pro ball for a Super Bowl-winning team and made major bank. Besides that, you're just like the rest of us."

The silver glint from one of the stones in my ring catches the sun as I walk. Yeah, I do love this bling, big-time. It almost takes the sting out of a too-short career on the gridiron.

"Anyway, *mildly argumentative sister of mine*—my point was not about Halloween candy but that the city is decked out in tinsel already," I say as I reach my building.

"Are you worried you're behind schedule if your tree's not up? You do know you don't have to start decorating in July like Mom does?"

On her end, a small voice calls out "Doggie," and my sister tells her son proudly, "Yes, Danny, that's the doggie."

"Doggie, bark," Danny says in the background.

I can't help but smile at her almost-two-year-old

cobbling short sentences together. "He wasn't saying 'bark' when I saw him last month."

"My child is clearly a genius."

"Just like his Uncle Vaughn."

"Yes, just like his uncle, since he's making trouble and encouraging the dog to bark."

"Good for him. Tell that little dude I cannot wait to see him while I'm there over Thanksgiving." I love that town, and I love Callie and my other sister Aubrey, and all my nephews and nieces. Both of my sisters' husbands are cool cats too.

"You're seriously the best for seeing him so often. Greg and I appreciate it."

"Like it's a hardship to make sure my nephew spends time with his favorite person."

"Goodbye, *cocky brother of mine.*"

"See you later." I hang up, then dart into the building, taking the steps two at a time up to our fifth-floor suite. Elevators can suck it.

Pushing open the door, I say hi to our receptionist then to my business partners, Haven, Josh, and Ford, before I head to my office, where I spend the day pacing the carpeted floor as I make work calls.

They go so damn swimmingly that I lob jump shot after jump shot in the net on the back of my office door as I talk.

"Slam dunk," I declare to no one after I negotiate a killer bonus clause for one of the Yankees.

Someone raps on my door. Opening it, I find Josh wearing his *I'm going to ask you for a favor* face.

I point at his grin. "Good thing you're not that transparent when negotiating. Are you going to ask me to pony up for an office pizza? Go halfsies on an espresso machine? Or maybe ask me to head up the Miami office we're opening in a few months?"

He wiggles his eyebrows. "Already got you on that one."

I grin broadly. "I know, and I'm psyched to head back to the beach. But what do you want me to do *today*?"

"Now why on earth would you think I'm about to hit you up?" He has the good sense to act surprised.

"You're easier to read than the Dallas D-line was back in my day."

He winces dramatically. "That hurts, man. Those guys were Swiss cheese."

"Don't I know it. It was awesome playing against them." I wave off the fond memories, then rub my palms together, ready to help my partner and friend. I'm always ready—that's my mantra. "Anyway, lay it on me. What do you need?"

"You know the holiday party we talked about having?"

"Of course."

"The good news is this: my sister Quinn says she'll plan it for us, and she has a couple of places she thinks we can still snag."

I park myself on the edge of my desk. "Does she not remember that you were a complete dick to her growing up?"

He scoffs. "I certainly was not. Also, how do you know how I was to my sisters when we were kids?"

"Let's see . . ." I scratch my head. "You're their older brother. Call it a lucky guess."

"I was an absolute angel as a child," he says with great dignity, then switches back to normal. "Anyway, I offered to pay her full rate, but she says it's her Christmas present to us, and even though I am the reigning king of negotiations, the one person I can't argue with is Quinn."

"Why's that?"

"She's relentless. Wiped the floor with us in Risk and Battleship. She could starve out your army in a siege of attrition, all with a smile to melt an ice-cold heart. Anyway, I was hoping you could join us for dinner tonight to chat about the party? Just to get the ball rolling."

"So she can wear me down too? I'm not a pushover like you, Summers."

"I wanted to include you because I thought it'd be right in your wheelhouse." He clears his throat, shifting into full-on flattery mode. "Since you're the most people-y of all of us."

I arch a brow. "*People-y*? One, not a word. Two, not sure it's flattering."

"It should be a word, and it's totally a compliment. It's your special skill."

"Since you suck at socializing?" I tease.

At least he owns it. "If it were up to me, I'd never go to a party again. But you're a social beast master."

"Again, not sure how to take that."

He places his hand flat over his heart. "With my most sincere admiration."

"Really? 'Beast' is a compliment?"

With an aggrieved sigh, he says, "Don't make me be nice."

"Do it," I goad, motioning with curling fingers for him to bring it on. "C'mon. I'm dying to see your nice routine. I've heard so much about it."

He huffs. "You're affable. You're easygoing. And I hate parties, so I need you, man. Besides, it's just one dinner. That's all."

"Aww. So sweet. That's all you had to say." I raise a finger, reconsidering. "Wait, let me amend that. Say, 'Vaughn, you rock at being the public face of this agency because you're so goddamn friendly and easy on the eyes.'"

He flips me the bird.

"Now *that* I'll take as a compliment."

* * *

That evening, we head to a nearby restaurant. Once inside, my gaze drifts to a woman with flaming-red hair at a booth in the back. Just as I think *Nice*, she waves to Josh, a picture-perfect smile lighting up her face.

Her *pretty* face. It seems Josh failed to mention that his sister is beautiful.

He was right about her smile though. It's melting something ice-cold in me . . . Not my heart.

My resolve.

Seriously?

I'd curse Father Christmas if that weren't blasphemy. Because are you kidding me? Why does my business partner's sister have to be a gorgeous redhead?

I have a thing for redheads. Especially fun, kind, witty, and flirty redheads.

What are the chances that she's going to hit the mark on each count?

No way. Not possible.

She probably hates kids and sports and laughter and snow and caroling, and hell, even puppies, making it that much easier for me to stick to my diet through this dinner. Yep.

With that pep talk, I follow my partner to the booth, ready to resist temptation.

When we reach the table, Josh makes quick introductions. "Vaughn, meet Quinn, my favorite sister, and I'm not just saying that because she worshiped me in high school and cheered the loudest at my games."

I groan inside. *She loves sports. Dammit.*

Quinn rises, punching Josh's arm. "You revisionist historian. I cheered the loudest because I was the head cheerleader."

*Double groan. That probably means she's outgoing.*

She meets my gaze, flashing a megawatt smile that belongs on the red carpet and in private corners of darkened rooms, and hell, do I ever love that smile already.

I offer a hand, and we shake. *Friendly, Vaughn. Just keep it friendly.*

"Great to meet you, Quinn. Funny thing. On the way over, Josh mentioned he lost a five-hundred-dollar bet to you recently and forgot to pay up—" My eyes go wide, swinging from Josh to Quinn. "Oh, my bad. That wasn't a secret, was it, man?"

Josh rolls his eyes then claps my shoulder. "And this is Vaughn. He loves to get my goat."

Quinn laughs. "What do you know, Vaughn? We have that in common. Also," she says to me with an approving glint in her green eyes, "when I finagle that five hundred bucks from him, we'll split it on VIP tickets to the amusement park. Maybe add in Skee-Ball and mini-golf too. Deal?"

"That sounds more than fair," I say, and I don't give away that I'm freaking out inside.

*Fun.* Check.

More fun than mini-golf, Skee-Ball, and amusement parks.

Which means I'm pretty much screwed.

## 2

# VAUGHN

At least Josh is here as a buffer.

Maybe with my business partner at the table, I'll think about what's at stake rather than his sister's pretty pink lips, the constellation of freckles dotting the bridge of her nose, or the mesmerizing curtain of her silky red hair.

Since I'm already liking her personality, I could use the willpower boost. With all I need to do before I leave town in less than two months, I don't need the distraction of a romance before I jet. Especially a no-go romance.

Josh's phone pings, and he checks out the screen. "I need to deal with this. Hope you two don't mind, but I'll be right back."

And so much for that strategy.

Josh leaves as Quinn sits. I slide into the booth across from her, careful not to smack my head on the low-hanging lamp over the table.

"I take it that's not your first encounter with a

lighting fixture that's out to get you?" she asks with a quirk of her lips.

"More like my ten-thousandth. And after countless run-ins over the years with vicious chandeliers, I learned to hone my ducking reflexes."

"Hazards of being as tall as a redwood tree, I suppose. But do the benefits outweigh the dangers?" She gives a sassy little lift of her eyebrow, and my pulse speeds up.

"Definitely. I'm in the supermarket helping little old ladies reach tall shelves all the time." There. Elderly shoppers who can't reach the prune juice. That image will settle things down.

"It's practically your superpower."

"All I need is a spandex shirt with a *T* for Tall logo, and I'm good to go."

She taps her chin, humming. "Maybe that's what I'll get you for Christmas."

"I'm on the present list already? That is excellent news. And if you ever need someone to reach the pickles on the highest shelf in the store, just dial *T* on your phone." I pat myself on the back. Look at me being friendly. This is hardly flirting at all.

"Actually, can I borrow you when I decorate my tree? Maybe you could do all the highest branches and I can finally have a tree that reaches the ceiling. That's a fantasy come true."

*And she likes Christmas. Man down. Man officially down.*

It's not like I can step away now, so I say, "Count me in. I love tree trimming. I love Christmas."

"You do?" she asks, musing.

"Yes. Everything from the mistletoe to the carols."

"I love carols," she agrees. "'The Christmas Song' is my favorite."

One more thing we have in common. I like that.

I like her. That's the trouble. Our dinner is speeding into feels-like-a-date territory.

"So, tell me more about your party-planning business," I say, valiantly steering the ship away from flirtier shores. "I'm coming into this blind and don't know much about it."

She drops her jaw, exaggerating outrage. "No! You're a pantser!"

Laughing, I ask, "What does that mean?"

"As in, fly-by-the-seat-of-your." Inching closer, she says, "I'm the opposite. A total researcher. A look-every-thing-up-er."

"That's a way to put it, I guess." Amused, I consider the word. It's a fair assessment. "You might be right. I do my homework, it's just that improvising doesn't scare me. Throw me into the fray, and I'll see what comes of it."

She shudders melodramatically. "I have no idea what that's like."

"Try it sometime. Maybe you'll like it." Yeah, I'm no good at being all business with Quinn.

"Not if I can help it," she says, shaking her head emphatically.

"So how far does this planning fascination of yours extend?"

"Far and wide." She points at me, leans closer, and

drops to a whisper. "Confession: I looked you up online before dinner."

That doesn't help my resolve, that sexy little feather of a voice she's put on. "And you still showed up. You're a brave woman," I say. Maybe some self-deprecation will slow this train for me.

"Please. Your team photos are great. You don't look that different from your Renegades pictures at all."

"Thanks." I run a hand through my hair. "It was only three years ago, and I haven't gained too much gray since."

"Yeah, but the wrinkles. All those wrinkles. Such a bummer," she says, deadpan.

I laugh. "It's hard being almost thirty."

She groans. "Then I should tell you that you have a great smile in photos, and in person too."

"Thank you. The same goes for you." I take a beat. "Well, I can only vouch for your in-person smile, since I'm not a stalker like someone else at this table." I shift my eyes back and forth, then land on her, giving her a knowing look. "But I'm not naming names."

She laughs, then brings her finger to her lips. "Thanks for keeping my dirty little secret."

This is going to be one hell of a battle. The woman is sweet and ridiculously friendly, as well as deliciously flirty.

But I'm determined to stick to my diet, so I focus on the reason we're here tonight. I drum my palms on the table to mark the topic shift. "So . . . Christmas parties, holiday fiestas, I'm your man. Christmas and I go way back. I'm a bit of an aficionado, I must admit."

"Is that so? Do you have a collection of reindeer sweaters I should know about? A secret penchant for baking Christmas cookies late at night?"

"Who said it was a secret? Maybe I'm completely out in the open about my Christmas baking."

She laughs like the chime of bells, and it's so damn adorable. "Do you have those little cookie cutouts and a cute Christmas apron?"

"Yes, and I wear a red sweater with a Rudolph nose on it while I make spiced fruitcake."

Her nose crinkles. "You didn't just say that."

I wink at her. "Just making sure you're paying attention. I don't hate anyone enough to give them fruitcakes. But I do make a most excellent gingerbread house." I preen a little, then lean closer to let her in on a secret. "In fact, I don't share this with just everyone, but I did win a gingerbread house contest when I was twelve."

"Shut the front door. We are definitely going to feature your gingerbread skills at the party, then. In fact, I would pay good money to see you making gingerbread houses in that sweater."

"Please. I don't accept monetary compensation. However, you're welcome to join me in putting the gumdrops on my culinary creation."

She clasps her hand to her chest. "I'm invited to the baking fiesta? Lucky me."

"As long as you bring the spiked hot chocolate."

"As if I'd bring any beverages that weren't spiked," she says, a wicked look in her eyes.

"So you're a naughty Christmas elf?"

"Hmm. Considering my childhood antics, I'd have to say yes."

"You can't drop a little nugget like that and not tell me more." I wiggle my fingers, beckoning her to give it up. "Childhood antics—what were they?"

She shakes her head and zips her lips. "Nope. Another time."

"Not fair. I told you about my ugly Christmas sweaters, as well as my gingerbread house skills."

She arches a skeptical brow. "You don't really have an ugly Christmas sweater collection, do you?"

"Maybe I do. Maybe I don't. Maybe you need to tell me why you deserved coal in your stocking."

She scans the restaurant for spies, then cups her mouth and whispers, "I used to peek at my presents."

My jaw drops. "That's an affront to all that is good in the holiday season. You definitely belong on the naughty list."

Her lips curve up in the tantalizing start of a grin. "Yeah, I kind of do."

I'm about ready to wave the white flag.

I'm *this close* to breaking my diet.

To asking her out on a date.

But Josh's return saves me.

"Sorry about that. Had to put out a fire. Everything good here?"

Quinn looks at me, still with that sliver of a smile. "Everything's great."

"Excellent. Glad to see you're getting along," he says.

"We're definitely getting along," I add, trying to take my eyes off Quinn.

But that's no easy feat, and it's a damn good thing Josh returned when he did.

We order our food, and as we eat and bat around ideas for the party, in the back of my mind, I cringe at how self-congratulatory I was when I walked into the office this morning. That was before Quinn Summers, who is shaping up to be the toughest temptation I've faced since I started my fast.

Good thing this is only one dinner.

# 3

# QUINN

It's not that I want my brother to leave.

It's that I *really* want my brother to leave.

And I love Josh madly.

But after the waitress pours the wine, his phone bleats for the twenty millionth time, and I honestly could kick him out of the booth just then.

*Happily.*

"You're in demand tonight," I say. "You can take the call. I won't be upset." He knows I'm not a phone person during meals. I'm not afraid to use the "do not disturb" setting, and I use it liberally.

But that's not why I want him to go.

"Sorry, guys. It's Enrique again. He's stressing out over something the Dodgers' GM said," Josh explains, waving the phone.

"Go. Take care of our guy," Vaughn says. I love the affectionate way he talks about their clients.

"Thanks. I'll be back after I triage this sitch." He takes off, weaving through the tables and out the door to chat on the street.

Good.

I'm alone with Vaughn again, and he is better than his pictures. His dark eyes twinkle, and his smile is magnetic, inviting, and . . .

*Stop!*

None of this is a surprise.

I thought I'd prepared for the onslaught of hotness with my immersion therapy—checking out all his pictures before dinner should have made me immune, or at least resistant, to him.

But just to be safe, I also didn't shave my legs tonight, and that guarantees that nothing can happen.

Not that anything *would* happen.

I doubt he's into me, plus my brother's here, plus this is business.

But even so, I need all the help I can get. The man is funny and friendly and so easy to talk to. Now that Josh is gone again, I need to focus on the holiday party so I don't stray toward temptation.

"So, you've drawn the short straw," I say. "They've roped you into Christmas party planning."

He smiles, a crooked grin that makes my chest zip and zing. "Is it the short straw though?" he asks, lifting his glass of wine and taking a drink.

"Considering how deeply my brother despises parties, I assume you two had a bet and you lost, and that's why you're here."

"Why would you think I'd lose? Maybe I'm excellent at wagers."

"Are you?"

He reaches into his wallet, fishes out a ten, and spreads it flat on the table. "I'm betting no one can convince me to serve eggnog at this party."

My eyes pop. "Why not? Eggnog is a staple at holiday parties."

"It is. And I need to know why, what we can do to avoid it, and if it can be stopped."

I laugh, taking a sip of my own wine. "I didn't realize there were eggnog haters."

He shakes his head. "I'm not an eggnog hater. I'm not a hater, period. I'm a lover."

Oh God, the way he says that word, like it tastes good on his tongue, sends a wave of inappropriate lust rolling over me. And now I'm wondering what kind of lover he is. Slow and tender? Rough and hungry? Devoted and attentive?

All of the above?

A girl can dream. But that doesn't mean she should.

*Focus, Quinn.*

"But not an eggnog lover?" I ask, getting back on track.

He leans a little closer, his big body occupying so much space. I'm not a small woman—I snagged the same tall genes that Josh did. But even at five nine, I feel like a pip-squeak next to the sequoia of Vaughn. I bet he's six foot five. Six foot *delicious* five. My stomach swoops as I watch him, how at ease he seems to feel in his body, the laid-back way he talks.

"Maybe I could grow to love eggnog, but I don't understand it."

"What's not to understand? It's creamy, a little spicy, a little sweet."

His lips hook into a grin. "Sure. True. But why do we need it? It just seems like the bastard stepchild of delicious holiday drinks."

"I noticed you didn't say the redheaded stepchild."

His gaze roams over my hair. "Now why on earth would I say that?"

"Is that because of the present company?" I flick some red strands over my shoulder.

"One, I would never say that. Two, I don't think I would ever compare you to eggnog."

"Oh, thank you," I say, laughing. "I guess that's a nightmare I never realized I had—being compared to eggnog." I take a beat, and the self-preservation part of me tells me sternly that I shouldn't be chatting like this, punctuating everything with a wink and a nod. I know I shouldn't flirt, and God knows I shouldn't take the next step.

But since I met him an hour ago, my heart has been tripping the light fantastic inside of me. I love a good old-fashioned conversation. And fine, maybe it is sprinkled with sugary flirtation. "What kind of drink would you compare me to, then?"

He takes his time studying me, and his gaze makes my skin sizzle. So much for my vow to stay unaffected.

Vaughn hums as he considers. "Vodka. Tequila. Whiskey. Something that has a little kick. What do you think?"

A wave of desire rolls down my spine.

His hot gaze is doing things to me I didn't expect.

Things I don't walk away from, even though I should. Instead of being professional, instead of keeping conversation to the party I've been hired to plan, I let it stray onto the what-kind-of-drink-am-I path. "I think I'm a tequila kind of woman."

"And that's the kind of drink you order a second round of," he says in a raspy, sexy tone.

My throat goes dry.

My libido speeds into overdrive.

And all my good sense slinks away.

I don't know where the hell it went, or if I want to find it.

And when my brother returns at last, I don't know if I want to throw my arms around him and thank him or kick him out the door.

But that's not a choice I can make, since he redirects the conversation to the reason we're here tonight—the holiday fete.

We're all business for the rest of the meal, Vaughn and I trading ideas, tossing out suggestions, and even arguing over the best Christmas songs, the ideal cocktails, and the most fantastic party games, until Josh smiles like a cat who snacked on a plate full of canaries.

My brother catches Vaughn's glance. "Turns out I need to take off for a week to deal with Enrique and some of the Los Angeles clients. What would you say to working with Quinn on the party details? You're much better at it than anyone else."

But he doesn't even need to butter him up, it seems. Vaughn catches my gaze, grins, then says, "Sure. I'd be happy to."

"Quinn, is that cool with you?" Josh asks. *Is he secretly trying to set me up with Vaughn?*

But I dismiss that thought. My brother is not the matchmaker type. He is definitely the party-hating type, and the busy type, so I know his question is legit.

And so is the answer I'm going to give.

Though I'm dating my job exclusively, I jump at the chance to spend time with this man—jump on it like it's a winning lottery ticket. "Want to start this weekend?"

Vaughn says yes, and we exchange phone numbers.

Oh, yes. Spending time with this wildly attractive man is a brilliant idea when I've sworn off romance.

# 4

## QUINN

As I turn over the card I've drawn in Pandemic, Amy and I groan in unison.

"Are you kidding me?" I say. "New York has another infection?"

"Board game epidemics are no laughing matter," my younger sister says soberly, and we set to work on finding a cure.

It's Friday night, and while we save the human race from deadly diseases at our favorite board game café, I ask what she's up to this weekend.

"I only have about six hundred manuscripts to read," she says with a too-bright smile.

"Only six hundred? That's less than last weekend, then." Amy's a junior editor at a publishing house and is working hard to move up the ladder.

"Look at you—always seeing the bright side."

"Also, if you have so many pages to edit, why are you hanging out with me on a Friday night?"

"Because Peyton and Lola are busy," she says matter-of-factly.

I huff indignantly and raise my game piece as if I'm going to bonk her with it. "And I love you too. Thanks for letting me know you'd rather be with your besties than me."

"Just kidding. You were my third choice," she says. "After my dog. But he had a hot date with a lady dog down the hall. I swear, he's such a dog-whore."

I roll my eyes. "At least I'm not your fourth choice after washing your socks."

"I laundered them last night. And I have the entire day tomorrow and Sunday to discover the next great novel. So that means I get to hang out with you in between socks and the slush pile."

"I feel so wanted. So loved."

"And what are you up to after we save the world?"

I have to rein in a secret smile when I say, "Just seeing Vaughn tomorrow night. We're planning a holiday party."

Amy arches a brow, all the way over the top of her red glasses. "Josh's business partner?"

"Yes." I keep my voice as even as I can, doing my best to strip out any shred of excitement or anticipation.

"On a Saturday night?"

"Yes. What's wrong with a Saturday night?"

She purses her lips then shrugs ever so innocently. "Gee. I don't know. Except it's a date night."

"We're simply checking out locations."

"Sounds like a date to me."

"It's not a date," I insist. She has it all wrong. She's just Amy being Amy—crafting a story when there's nothing there. "We're scoping out venues for a party. That is all. We arranged it as a work thing."

She wiggles her fingers. "Give me your phone."

I scoff. "So you can text him and ask if he thinks it's a date when I told you it's not?"

"Who? Me? Never."

"I know you, Amy. You're a little stinker."

She lifts her chin defiantly. "At least I didn't open my presents before Christmas."

I drop my jaw. "You knew about that?"

She stares me down pointedly. "We all did."

I square my shoulders and draw another card in the game. "I just like to be prepared."

"In that case, you should find out if he thinks it's a date."

I stare sharply at my sister. "I'm *not* asking him if he thinks it's a date when I know it's not a date. I know it, and he knows it, and you should know it too."

"You know Josh would never care that you were into his business partner," Amy adds, like she's laying a trail of breadcrumbs, yummy ones that lead to Vaughn.

My lips are ruler-straight when I answer her. "I know. He's not like that, and besides, we Summers women make our own choices about who we date. But for the ten-millionth time, it is not a date." I flap my hand at the board. "Now, let's save the world."

But still, her words badger me later that night, reminding me of the value of certainty. It can't hurt to reach out and confirm our plans. Our non-date plans.

Our very work-centric plans.

Later that evening I send the man a text, keeping my tone businesslike.

**Quinn:** Hi there! Just wanted to let you know I've researched some venues for us to visit tomorrow evening.

**Vaughn:** Excellent. You're such a planner. :)

**Quinn:** Ha! That's my job! That's literally what you hired me to do.

**Vaughn:** What? We hired you? Now you're trying to surprise me.

**Quinn:** Oh, ha ha ha. Way to take advantage of my weakness.

**Vaughn:** Nah. I bet your prepper nature is your strength. And I'm down with all of this. Tomorrow night sounds good.

**Quinn:** Thank you. I didn't make appointments because I think it'll be good for us to see what the places are like au naturel.

**Vaughn:** Isn't that the best way to check things out? ;)

My eyes pop.

Did he really just write that?

I rub my eyes and read it again.

Yes. Yes, he did.

He's a little flirty, possibly dirty, and I need to slam on the brakes.

So I do my best with a professional reply.

**Quinn:** Great. So we'll check out the three places I'm emailing you now. I'll meet you at the first one, and then we'll be all set.

There. I've established the plan. Set the boundaries. The man who tantalizes me won't be able to tempt me tomorrow.

**Vaughn:** Or we could throw the playbook out the window and wander into random establishments.

**Quinn:** I know what you're doing, and you're very naughty.

**Vaughn:** Yes, I'm the naughtiest. Forgive me for trying to shock your plan-loving heart.

**Quinn:** I'll forgive you. For now.

. . .

I may have set the boundaries, but I still want to break them. Vaughn and I had instant chemistry the other night, the kind of delicious connection that doesn't come around often.

But that's the problem. Connections lead to intimacy, and intimacy leads to heartbreak.

I shut my eyes and let my mind return to my last boyfriend. Clarke and I were together for a year, and just as I was about to move in with him, he announced —at my birthday dinner, no less—that he'd had a revelation.

He was in love with his ex-wife and had decided to try again with her.

Surprise!

Unhappy birthday to me.

I'd been shocked and broken. All my plans capsized.

So I poured my heart into my business because my business couldn't leave me for someone else.

No one will blindside me again.

I can't handle that kind of hurt, so I'll avoid the possibility entirely.

That's what I remind myself when I shove all my sister's loony ideas out of my head.

The next night I wade through my closet, considering the best outfit to wear for the meeting.

My favorite jeans and that cute green top?

Or maybe the red skirt that fits just so?

I tap my chin, noodling on the options.

Ooh, those black boots are great for chilly weather.

I try them with the jeans, with the skirt, then with a dress, and decide on the skirt and the boots.

As I shower, I review the venues one more time, picturing each place, preparing to shift into full-on party planner mode.

Still, even party planners could use a shave . . .

# VAUGHN

I haven't broken my guidelines.

I haven't even bent them.

The dinner with Quinn the other night was merely a momentary flirtation, a few accidentally naughty comments.

Well, maybe not *entirely* accidental.

But there were only a couple.

Hell, if I was *that* tempted to fall off the wagon, I'd simply remove the opportunity. I'd can our venue recon plan and schedule a simple phone call instead.

But I can handle being near her, even without Josh as a safety net. Even without the hard deadline of jetting out of Manhattan at the start of the new year to expand our firm and open the Miami offices of Premiere.

And if I waver, there's the still-fresh memory of Lexi reminding me why I laid down the law in the first place. My ex was dangerous and delicious, a combination that was my downfall with her. She convinced me to jump ship from the first agency I worked at to a company headed by Dick Blaine.

When I wanted to walk away after Dick asked me to do something unethical—make sure every single client had a fall guy, a friend who could take the rap if an athlete was driving drunk or screwing prostitutes—Lexi said I should stay. And that we should get married.

That was when the light bulb went on—she'd hitched her star to mine, figuring I was on the path to making more dough with Dick.

It's easy to dislike Lexi in hindsight. But then I'd have to dislike myself because I was in love with her.

Or so I thought.

Hard to say now if it was love, or if I was simply a fool. All I know is I don't want to get hoodwinked again.

That's why romance is off the menu.

When it's time to see Quinn on Saturday, I say my ex's name like a talisman as I button my shirt, roll up my cuffs, and check out my reflection. "Don't forget Lexi," I tell the guy in the mirror. "And whatever else, don't forget this isn't a date."

I meet Quinn on a block in Gramercy Park, telling myself I'm not thinking about her pink lips, or her green eyes, or the cute little red skirt and black boots she's wearing.

Nope. We're total professionals as we embark on our quest to check out venues for the party.

The first is a trendy lounge with a fireplace and

fantastic cocktails. It's a decent choice with a fun vibe. "This is a good one. I can see us having a party here."

"Exactly! It's a great size for the guest list, and it has a cozy holiday feel to it at the same time," she says, sinking onto a couch and stroking her chin. "I see Yule logs, fruitcake, and eggnog."

I flop down next to her, narrowing my eyes. "Nope. I imagine a cranberry old-fashioned, a candy cane cocktail, and peppermint martinis."

"Just teasing. I would never put eggnog on the menu with you." She lowers her voice. "Eggnog hater."

"Hey now," I say, indignant. "I just want to give the underserved cocktails their time in the limelight."

She lifts one brow. "Question though. What exactly is a candy cane cocktail?"

I laugh, shrugging because I have no clue. "Just made that up. But we should invent one and serve it. Everyone will speak for years about the delicious drinks we mixed up."

She nods, her brow knit like she's figuring me out. "I get you. You're looking to shake things up. I've got your number, Vaughn."

*Does she ever.* "Yes, you absolutely have my number," I say, my voice going low and a little raspy.

She tilts her head to meet my gaze, and our faces are inches apart. "Yeah?"

"You do."

The question and the answer hang in the air like smoke.

We're both quiet for a few seconds, maybe more. The space between us feels charged, electric, full of things unsaid. I wait for her to respond, but I'm not even sure what I want her to say or do.

Except I am.

I want her to tell me that she feels this too.

And though I should look away, should break the connection, I don't. I like looking at her far too much.

She clears her throat, runs her hands down her thighs, then glances toward the bar before turning back. "So, we keep this place on the short list. And we add candy cane cocktails."

"Definitely," I say, but maybe I read the whole night wrong.

Maybe she has my number, but I don't have hers.

# 6

## VAUGHN

We leave the lounge, and I vow to shake off the date vibe.

This is not a date.

It's exactly what it's supposed to be—a business meeting on a Saturday night, because Saturday night is when you scout party locations.

Besides, Quinn seems focused on keeping everything professional.

As we walk to the next spot, she asks, "What do you like most about your client list?"

This is good—concentrate on the work connection. Plus, I like her question. "For starters, they're top talent. I absolutely love working with overachievers."

"Definitely. Because then they inspire you too."

I smile, loving that she gets it. "Yes. When they're committed to giving all on the field, it drives me to do even better for them."

"And you've always been driven," she says, lifting a finger to make a point as we reach the crosswalk. "Well,

I presume so. You don't get to the Super Bowl without being driven."

I gesture to her. "Or become one of New York's best event planners."

She stops in her tracks, grabs my elbow, and cracks up. "Oh my God, you're hilarious."

"What's so funny?"

"Did you really just compare what I do to what you do? You're a sweetheart, but you don't have to say that."

I shoot her a confused look. "I meant it as a compliment. A legit compliment."

"Oh, sure. I'm the Tom Brady of party planners," she says with a straight face.

"Quinn, don't sell yourself short. I looked you up after we met, and you have insane online reviews."

Her green eyes seem to twinkle, maybe with surprise. "You did?"

I nod, owning it. "Didn't expect that, did you?"

She purses her lips, then shakes her head, like she's reining in a smile. "Really? But still, you don't have to compare me to top athletes."

"Why not? You're top in your field. And want to know what else I learned when I looked you up?"

"Maybe . . .?"

I point at her, at this gorgeous, confident, kind woman standing beneath a string of icicle lights on a New York street corner. "Your clients love you. The things they've said about you in reviews are terrific. You should be proud of what you've built."

Her smile is as wide as the city block, as bright as

the Christmas lights in the shop window. "Thank you. I'm completely flattered."

"I was impressed." As we resume our pace, I rattle off more of what her clients said online. "*I cannot even begin to express how happy I am that we hired Quinn.* That was one. *She's thorough, organized, calm, and an utter delight.* And another said, *The party was amazing, thanks to Quinn. Also, she's naturally festive.*"

"I can't believe you found all that," she says softly. A faint blush sneaks across her cheeks as we turn onto the next block.

"Am I embarrassing you?"

She shakes her head, her eyes widening. "No. It's just sort of . . . unexpected. I don't think I've ever been complimented on my business by someone—"

She cuts herself off, and I'm not sure how she was planning on finishing that sentence, but I'm sure of what I want her to say—*by someone I'm interested in.*

That's the problem.

Try as I might to deny and resist, I want her to feel the same unexpected attraction to me as I do to her.

I want her to grab my shirt, meet my gaze with fire in her eyes, and say, *You know what, Vaughn? You're great, and I'd like you to take me home tonight and make sure I'm nowhere this year but on the naughty list.*

And I'd reply, *Consider it done.*

Then on Monday, I'd give her brother a courtesy heads-up. That's how you do these things. If you date your business partner's sister, you let him know.

But that's not what's happening.

Instead, I return to the topic of work, hoping it will

return the focus to the reason we're here. "How did you wind up in event planning? Is it because—wild guess—you like to plan?"

She shakes her head. "I like making people happy. Parties and gatherings usually do that. That's what I love—I want to bring the feel-good factor to the lives of others."

That doesn't help my situation. Because her answer makes my heart thump. I like it too much. "You're the opposite of a process server, then. You bring good news."

She laughs deeply, reaching for my arm again. "I suppose if I really wanted to deliver happiness, I should have been a stork."

Now I crack up. "That's a good gig, I'll bet."

When we reach the swank restaurant, we focus on the mission and check out a private room in the back. The decor is sleek and modern, a vivid contrast to the last place.

She sweeps her hand to showcase the room, once again in planner mode. "It's simple but elegant. And if you want a holiday theme, we can set up a few small trees and decorate them, or simply hang wreaths and other seasonal decor on the wall. Also, since you mentioned fun drinks and food, I think you'll like this idea I have. What if we did a hot chocolate bar and a cookie-decorating station? You said you want your clients to be able to bring their kids and family. This space is ideal for it."

I mime an explosion with my fingers. "Stop. That's too perfect."

Her smile ignites. "You like it?"

I tap my chest. "Well, for me. We can do the hot chocolate bar solely for me. Forget about the clients."

"Got a little sweet tooth?"

I hold up a thumb and forefinger. "Just a tiny one."

"Then I insist on the hot chocolate bar."

"Insist. Please."

She points to the far wall. "Right there. I can see it now."

"What I see is a hot chocolate taste-test in my future."

She nudges me with her elbow. "Shh. That's on tomorrow night's agenda."

*Tomorrow night.*

My ears perk up. Hell, everything perks up. Are we having a tomorrow night?

But now isn't the time to ask. She turns around, taking in the spacious room. "I bet the acoustics here are good too. Imagine how Nat King Cole would sound crooning 'The Christmas Song.'"

"You can't go wrong with chestnuts roasting on an open fire."

A happy sigh falls from her lips. "But I also love 'Have Yourself a Merry Little Christmas.' Even though that song is kind of sad. Confession: I play that year-round when I'm feeling blue."

"What happened the last time you played it?" I ask, curious what would get this cheery woman down.

She waves a hand, dismissing it. "Oh, it was nothing. Not worth mentioning."

Crossing my arms, I go all gruff badass. "Nope. It's

not nothing. Who is he and should I kick his ass now or later?" I mean it as a joke, but I hate the thought of some guy hurting her. Despise it, in fact. "Did someone hurt you?"

She swallows and looks away briefly, then back at me. "My ex, when he left me to get back with his first wife. But it was a year ago, and I've been focused on business since then. I don't think about him, and I'm not sad anymore."

"Good," I say emphatically, stepping closer to her. "Because he doesn't deserve you."

She lifts her chin, eyeing me curiously. "Why do you say that?"

"Any man who'd walk away from you doesn't deserve you."

She licks her lips then says softly, "Thank you. That's kind of you to say."

"I'm not saying it just to be nice. I'm saying it because it's true." I don't know how I've gotten here, so close to telling her I think she's fantastic, especially since I have no idea whether she's on the same page as me.

But something about Quinn—hell, *everything* about her—just does it for me.

Her humor, her honesty, her bright outlook.

And another thing about her—us—that works for me is our chemistry. We seem to have a certain connection. It's come on quickly and taken me by surprise.

I should hit stop but instead I open up and take a dive into the ex waters. "I haven't played a sad song since things ended with my ex either."

She narrows her eyes and raises her fists. "Want me to go pull her hair and scratch her eyes out?"

I laugh, loving the tigress in her. "Nah, it's all for the best. I'm happier without her. Things ended months ago. She was more interested in my wallet than me."

Her lip curls and she issues a disgusted *ugh*. "She's the one missing out."

There's a glimmer there of something that perhaps I *was* seeking after all—the hint that this is a two-way street.

"I've been all about work since then too. And I'm better off without her."

"I'm better off without him," she seconds, a smile teasing at her lips.

We echo each other even in talking about our pasts. This feels all too right—the honesty, the openness, the admissions.

"Then there's no need to play a sad song," I add, "even though that's a damn good tune."

She leans a little closer, her shoulder brushing mine. "It is a good song. But it's no 'Frosty the Snowman.'" Her laugh is a little flirty, and hell, do I like that sound.

"You can't go wrong with Frosty," I say as she reaches for her phone and taps a few buttons, then the opening notes of the tune begin to play.

"It's official. We're playing only happy tunes at the party, we're getting a Skee-Ball machine decked out in holly, and we're having a hot chocolate bar."

She grabs my arm, squeezing it, and all I can think

is *Oh, this is what we're doing? We're already touching each other? Merry Christmas to me.*

"I love literally everything about that. But we have one more place to check out." She wags an admonishing finger at me. "Don't think you can cut the night short."

I gaze into her lovely green eyes, pretty sure that I'm already a goner for her. "The last thing I want to do is to call it a night before we have to."

"Then don't," she whispers.

I'm hanging on to resistance by a thread, and a part of me doesn't care why I was resisting in the first place.

We leave, and I have a feeling I do have her number now, and I want to keep it. The question is, what the hell am I going to do about that?

# 7

## VAUGHN

What am I going to do? The immediate answer is *go*.

As in, go to the third location.

We snag an Uber to take us to the Upper East Side. I open the door to the black Lexus, and as she slides in ahead of me, I'd like to say my gaze doesn't linger on her skirt, or her legs, or her boots.

But that'd be a lie.

I can't take my eyes off her.

I can't stop wondering how she smells, what kind of sounds she'd make if I touched her, if her hair would be as soft in my hands as I imagine.

"One more place," she tells me, sounding a bit wistful, as if she doesn't want the night to end. "Maybe the third time's a charm."

"I'd say the first two have been pretty damn charming."

"You sure know how to make an event planner feel like a rock star. I've never had a client who liked *all* the places I'd scoped out."

"First time for everything," I say as the car lurches down the street. "But what's your prediction, Miss Loves-to-Plan? Do you think the last one will shock, awe, and wow us?"

She taps my thigh. This woman is quite handsy, and I love it. "It only has to wow *you*."

"No way. I want you to be impressed. You're the expert. So, what do you think? Will this be the winner?"

She draws a deep breath, teasing as she says, "I don't know. Maybe I was taking you to two mediocre places, wanting to blow you away with this last one."

I narrow my eyes. "Ooh, so you're a tricky event planner."

"Of course. I used the old super-sneaky save-the-best-for-last trick."

"That is so sly. Maybe I need to get you a spandex T-shirt with an *S* logo for Christmas."

Her lips curve into a sneaky grin. "I'll peek under the tree."

"Just act surprised, then."

"I can definitely do that," she says, looking oh so satisfied. Then her tone turns questioning. "Vaughn . . .?"

"Yeah?"

Her voice is earnest, a little vulnerable, even. "Here's the funny thing. My brother said you're pretty easygoing, and I never entirely believe it when someone says that. But you are. And it's funny because I always thought of you as pretty intense when you played football."

This catches my attention. "You watched me play?"

I can't help a warm glow of pride. I was damn good on the field, and I like knowing this incredible woman enjoyed my games.

She shoots me a look. "Uh, yeah. Hello. Big-time football fan here. And I might have played a little fantasy football back in the day."

"I was your lucky charm, right?" I ask with a wink.

"No, I traded you," she deadpans.

I groan and clutch my heart where she just stabbed me. "Oh, the anguish. I'm utterly devastated."

Laughing, she nudges my elbow. "Just kidding. Actually, I picked you up for a small amount, and you were definitely an outperformer."

I blow on my fingernails then buff them on my chest. "It's always good to exceed expectations."

"Right? I'd rather surprise people than disappoint them."

"And you said you hated surprises."

"I hate being surprised," she explains. "I love surprising others."

"I'll make a mental note to always give you an unmissable heads-up about everything."

"Yes, please do that. But don't distract me—we were talking about you. I remember you having this intensity when you played. You were like a tiger, ready to pounce," she says as the car pulls up at our destination.

We step out and head toward the entrance of a trendy boutique hotel.

"Honestly, that's one of the nicest things anyone's ever said to me," I tell her. She glances curiously at me as we walk. "The pouncing thing. That's truly what I aimed to do every time I was on the field."

"Do you wish you still played?"

I sigh heavily, a small pang in my heart. "For a few seconds when I think about it."

"Like now? Because I can see it in your eyes." She stops in front of me, gesturing to my face. "There's a hint of sadness."

"Hey now, I'm not a sad guy."

"I know that. I can tell already. But it's also okay if you miss something you loved madly."

"You don't devote two decades of your life to something if you don't love it deep in your bones." My emotions are close to the surface as I say it, but then I hold up my hand and give a *moving on* wave. "Most of the time, I'm simply happy I was able to do it at all. And I love, absolutely love, what I do now, especially since I'll be tasked with expanding the agency into Florida. I'm opening the Miami offices early next year."

"That's fantastic. That's such an important area to be in, with so many pro athletes in Florida."

"Exactly, plus my sisters are there, and my mom and dad. To say I'm excited about this next phase of my career would be an understatement."

She hums thoughtfully as we resume walking. "So, you reinvented yourself, and you're good with it."

"Exactly. I loved playing, but the ACL tear also gave me a chance to find something else I love doing. I'm lucky that way. I can't change things, so why wallow in regret? I'm simply glad I was able to play pro ball for the three years I did. It's a career most people just dream of having."

We reach the lobby doors and I open one for her. "That's such a refreshing attitude," she says as she goes in and I follow.

I shrug. "It's the only thing we can control. How we see things. How we respond. So, I choose to have a good attitude. And that's what makes me tick," I wrap up as we walk past the concierge. She nods hello to someone she must know well, but we continue on. "What about you, Miss Party Planner? What makes you tick, besides exhaustive research and meticulous planning?"

"What makes me happy in my job, you mean?"

"Just life in general. What's your jam?"

She mulls over the question, and a little smile quirks up the corner of her lips. "I do love people. Getting to know them, talking to them. I love music and sports and concerts. I like to look up the set list in advance so I know what order the band will play their songs."

I pretend to be shocked. "Wait. The Quinn picture is coming together. You peek at presents and you want to know what's coming next in a set list. I bet you look up the endings of movies too."

As we stroll down the hallway, she shoots me a side-eye, like the answer is obvious. "Of course I do."

"If I took you to see a comedian, would you watch their videos on YouTube beforehand?"

It sounds like I've asked her on a date, I realize. And I'm suddenly aware, too, that I *should*. Not just hypothetically. But an *actual* date.

Besides, I take off for Florida in less than two months. Maybe I can pull off an entanglement with limits. Like a cheat day on a diet. Then I'll return to the regimen after the binge.

"Of course," she answers as I marinate on that possibility.

"And it wouldn't bother you to know the jokes in advance?"

"God, no. I'd love it." Her nose crinkles adorably. "Is that weird?"

"No, it's kind of cute." It is and she is, and I should not enjoy this so much.

But I do.

And I don't want our time together to end, so I entertain the cheat day option even more.

She flashes me a smile, one that makes my blood heat. *This woman.* She is weaving her way under my skin and into my head in record time.

We reach the event room, and as soon as we step inside, I hold out a hand. "Stop."

She spins and meets my eyes, a question in hers. "What is it?"

"It's perfect. You are on the take," I accuse playfully.

She wiggles her brows. "Guilty as charged." But then she clasps her hands together. "Do you really like it?"

I look around, taking in the room. I'm not an expert, but it feels like the perfect venue. The size is ideal, and the brick walls seem warm and welcoming. Plus, it's pre-decorated with blue-and-white lights and a couple of wreaths. It feels like our firm—classy, fun, and never ostentatious.

"I do. And I dig that it's decorated."

"Is there anything better than Christmas decorations?"

I let out a long, low whistle. "As long as they don't go up in July."

"Wait. Is there a secret Christmas past you're hiding from me?" she asks, her tone drenched in curiosity.

I set a hand on her arm and take a deep breath. "We're going to need a drink for this conversation."

"Then I'd say it's time for cocktails, since I don't want to call it a night yet."

And I might be falling.

Oh hell, who am I kidding?

I'm falling so damn fast.

# 8

## QUINN

We head for the hotel bar, snagging a quiet booth in the corner where we park ourselves on a royal-blue cushioned couch and order.

After the waitress brings two vodka tonics, Vaughn takes a deep breath then runs his hands through his dark hair. "All right. Don't say I didn't warn you. Are you ready?"

I nearly bounce on the cushion. I'm dying to know. "Tell me, tell me, tell me."

"Ever wonder about those crazy Christmas houses in the neighborhood? You know the ones—where they start setting up in July, and every single room is decked out in a Christmas theme."

"Yes," I say, my eyes bugging out. "There was one like that where we grew up. We used to drive by and gawk at it every year."

His dark eyes twinkle. "And they're full of Christmas displays. Trains bringing toys to Santa's workshop. Small towns covered in snow."

"Reindeer across the lawn and a sleigh on the roof."

"And there are three, four, five . . . I could never keep count of how many Christmas trees we had set up in every room."

I don't say anything for a few seconds. Then the enormity of his statement registers. "Nooo. For real?" I'm so excited, I'm shaking. I've always wanted to know someone who lived in a crazy Christmas house. "You? You lived in one?"

He nods, solemn, as if we're in a confessional. "Every square inch of the lawn decorated in reindeers and giant snowmen. And sleighs . . . so many sleighs. There are candy canes everywhere. You can't escape them. And the price of admission to see inside helps support the extravagant electricity bill. That was my house growing up." He taps his broad, muscular chest. "My parents were, and still are, absolutely obsessed with Christmas."

I stifle a squeal. "You lucky duck. I would have loved a Christmas house."

"Are you sure?" he asks, taking a swallow of the vodka tonic.

"Didn't you? I'm sure there were moments when it was too much, but mostly it sounds like a blast for kids."

His smile spreads, slow and easy. "I'll admit it was kind of fun."

"See? I knew it. But how does something like that start? Where's your mom from, the North Pole?"

He laughs, shaking his head. "No, she was born in Thailand. Her dad is from Bangkok. Her mom is from

Portugal. My dad's family is all from Virginia, and my parents recently retired to Florida when Callie moved there, and Aubrey too."

"All right, so no members of your family are from the Arctic Circle."

"Nope. Not even close."

I scoot a little closer, enjoying getting to know him. Enjoying this whole night, in fact. Considering how well Vaughn and I clicked the first time we met, maybe it's no surprise how much I like spending time with him. And I've loved this whole business meeting so far, even when I wasn't quite sure how to respond over the whole "do I have your number" thing.

I hadn't known what to say because everything was happening faster than my defenses could handle. I still feel rushed along in a swift current, but I don't want it to stop. I feel like we could talk all night and it might not be enough.

"You didn't grow up hating Christmas?" I ask.

"Shocking, isn't it? You'd figure I'd loathe everything red and green, and I'd hate ornaments and sparkling lights."

"You're not that kind of guy." I feel a little warm and buzzy, and I'm not sure if it's from the vodka or from chatting with him.

Actually, that's a lie. I am sure.

It's from him.

Everything I'm feeling tonight is about him, for him, because of him. I'm warm all over. Wait—make that hot. My skin tingles at the way he looks at me with hunger in his deep brown eyes.

"I'm absolutely not a scrooge," he adds.

"You're the opposite. And I think you're also a what-you-see-is-what-you-get kind of guy." My throat's gone dry, so I take another drink.

He takes one too. "And how do you feel about that, Quinn?"

We're not talking about parties. Or Christmas houses. Or how we approach the world. We're talking about this crazy chemistry that's crackling undeniably after two dates.

I mean, two evenings together.

Both of which feel like dates.

Like wonderful, thrilling, *delicious* dates.

"I like it," I confess, then I zip my lips because I can't say more. My heart is on lockdown, but I'm so tempted to unlock it for him.

I promised myself. I don't want to date, don't want a relationship. I don't want to fall.

I can't handle getting hurt.

And the thing is, I could get hurt with him. Already I feel myself yielding—liking him, wanting him—more than I'm prepared for.

Except he's leaving New York, which puts a guaranteed expiration date on any hypothetical relationship. Could he truly hurt me in so narrow a window of time? It makes things safe, makes me impervious to heartache.

"And do we have a winner here in this hotel?" I ask, concentrating on the job I'm contracted to do with his firm. I gesture around the bar though the party will be in the room we checked out already.

He takes a breath, then nods. "Yeah, it's a winner. Let's have the party here."

As we finish our drinks, we chat about the party, the menu, and the Skee-Ball he wants to have at the soiree.

When we're done, we leave the bar and head toward the lobby, turning a corner. As we walk down the hall, my feet feel leaden, and my mood turns darker.

I don't want this time with him to end.

I stop decisively. "You know, we should talk more about the menu."

His eyes light up with possibility. "Absolutely. Do you want to meet again tomorrow? We can plan the hot chocolate bar and the appetizers, and we should figure out what the heck goes in a candy cane cocktail."

Somewhere inside me a warning bell sounds.

*You're not supposed to be dating. You're not supposed to date him. You're taking a dating break.*

But the way he looks at me, the way I feel for him, makes me shove those mantras I prepared out of the way.

Besides, we'd only be temporary. This is a chance my once-broken heart can afford to take. "True. Those are all vital details." I break into a wild grin because I feel crazy saying yes. But it's a good crazy.

"Then tomorrow we'll get to the bottom of it." His smile matches mine as his gaze drifts to the ceiling.

Curiosity takes mine there too.

A sprig of mistletoe hangs above the entryway at the end of the hall.

Oh hell, is that ever an invitation.

His eyes return to mine. "Should there be mistletoe at the party?"

"Shouldn't there always be mistletoe?" I say by way of an answer.

"The thing about mistletoe," he says, stepping closer, and my heart flutters, "is it's not a surprise. It gives you a heads-up: kisses may happen here."

"Are you giving me a heads-up?" I ask breathlessly.

"Do you want one?"

"I don't need one," I whisper. "I think I know what happens next."

"The only thing I want to happen." He dips his head, lowering his mouth, and dusts the softest, most tempting kiss against my lips.

I feel like I'm floating.

Like I'm flying.

For a few delicious seconds, he dives in, kissing with intent, leaving me with the promise of how his touch might be—thorough and attentive enough to make my toes curl.

He breaks the kiss, slides his hand around my head, and pulls me in close, inhaling deeply of my hair. "You're incredible. And that should come as no surprise."

We make our way out, and as he puts me in a car, he tucks my hair behind my ear and says in that sexy, raspy voice, "I don't want to keep you in suspense, so I'm just going to tell you now—I'm counting down the hours till tomorrow."

"Me too."

* * *

"And then he kissed me."

I take a sip of my coffee as I finish describing last night to my sister.

Amy sprawls dramatically in her chair at Dr. Insomnia's, swooning and fanning herself. "This is the best story ever. It's so good I don't even need a vanilla latte today."

"Seriously? You *always* need a vanilla latte."

She sits bolt upright. "I know, but a kiss under the mistletoe from a guy like him? Even better than a vanilla latte."

"Imagine if it happened to you," I say, since I'm feeling a little sass, fueled by Vaughn's fantastic kiss. "That would be better than cake *and* a latte."

She narrows her eyes. "You are evil for taunting me with your romantic escapades and then mocking me for my single-tude. But you were always the mean one."

"I'm awful, I know. But it was so wonderful." I sigh, unable to help myself. "It was the best first kiss in the history of kisses."

"I forgive you." My sister echoes my happy sigh, but then she frowns. "But what happens next? I thought you were abstaining from love and romance and dating thanks to Clarke's exhibition of epic douchery. Something about how you wanted to lock that organ up in a steel cage."

"I *am* off of dating," I say. Yes, my heart seems to frolic and sing around Vaughn, or even at the thought of Vaughn, but I've got this under control. With a solid plan A, I don't need a plan B. "But he's moving to Miami after the new year to open the offices there for Premiere, so we have built-in barriers. It can't turn into something more, so my heart can stay in its cage." I shrug, a little coquettishly. "A date here, a night there. What's the worst that could happen?"

She arches a knowing brow and stares pointedly at me. "I don't think you want me to answer that. Why don't you just tell me about the kiss again?"

I grin and happily tell the story one more time.

# 9

## VAUGHN

Like a game show host, my sister opens the fridge with a flourish. "See? It's perfect," she says via FaceTime. "There's nothing in it, and that's exactly how it'll look when you live here."

"O ye of little faith. I learned how to cook. I even have a recipe book."

"Yeah, full of menus from your favorite take-out spots."

"Please. Who needs menus? It's all on the apps now." I try to catch Danny's attention as he's running in circles in the kitchen of the condo I'm thinking of buying in Miami. My realtor just listed my apartment in Manhattan the other day, and I've already had offers.

"Danny, my man. Tell your mom she's disparaging your favorite person."

My nephew meets my gaze on the screen. "Vaughn barks!"

Callie cackles. "He just compared you to a dog."

I shrug because it's all good. "Dogs are cool. Danny, I accept your compliment."

"Vaughn flies!" He calls me by my name, since it's easier to say than "Uncle."

I point at the little dude with the apple cheeks. "See? You are a genius," I tell the rug rat before he scampers away from the phone. "He knows I'm coming to see him in a few weeks."

"And we can't wait," Callie says with a smile before she turns serious. "What do you think? Do you like this place? Aubrey and I both checked it out for you."

"It's pretty sweet," I say. "I could see myself in it. Plus, it's on the beach, and I love going for morning runs. Or evening runs. Or anytime runs."

"Being near the water is great. It's fantastic here."

I scratch my jaw, considering the place. "Let me think on it tonight. Wait. I won't think about it tonight. Because I have a date."

Her blue eyes spark. "Ooh, do tell."

I give her the briefest description of Quinn. "She's fantastic and warm, funny and beautiful. And I had a great time with her."

She hums. "Be careful, Vaughn."

"Why?"

"Because you fall easily and you're leaving town soon. You only have the holiday season."

A montage flicks before my eyes. Quinn and me, out and about in the city, strolling down Fifth Avenue as snow falls, skating in Rockefeller Center, setting up her tree. Then me distracting her from decorating with kisses that lead to the bedroom. Not a bad way to spend the next several weeks, come to think of it. "That means it'll all be fine. It won't hurt, since I know I have to leave."

Callie stares at me like my answer doesn't compute. "That's illogical. How does the duration prevent the pitfall?"

"Because there is an expiration date. No surprises, no promises, and no broken heart. It's brilliant. And so is the deal on that condo. I'll take it."

She blinks. "You decided already?"

"Yes. I can see myself in it. Can you tell the realtor I'll make an offer?" There's no point in delaying the purchase.

"Sure. And have fun tonight," she says with a smile. "As long as you're being careful."

"I will," I assure her.

But caution is not what I feel when I see Quinn.

What I feel when I meet Quinn outside of Lulu's Chocolates in the West Village is longing, desire, and anticipation.

Quinn's black boots click-clack on the sidewalk as she walks toward me, her red hair peeking out from under a green knit cap that's sexier than a knit cap should ever be.

But then, everything about her is sexy.

Everything about her makes my pulse race.

And everything about her makes me want to kiss her.

So that's what I do when she reaches me. I slide a hand around her waist and say "Hi," then dip my mouth to hers.

I surprise the hell out of her, and I love it, because when I break the kiss, her eyes are still shut and her lips are still parted.

It's the perfect look on the most tempting woman.

And I can't get her out of my head.

# 10

## VAUGHN

The salted caramel hot chocolate is sinful. The dark-as-night kind is decadent. And the spiked cocoa is insanely good. The splash of tequila, courtesy of a flask Quinn brandishes, is just the right touch.

"Here's my verdict for the party," I tell her as we survey the hot chocolates Lulu served us. "Let's have it all. Every single flavor."

Quinn nudges me with her shoulder. "You have quite an appetite."

"I'm just saying, this is all way better than eggnog."

Quinn lifts a finger. "Ah, but you haven't had Lulu's eggnog hot chocolate."

"Is that a thing?"

Quinn waves to the curly-haired blonde with the vibrant green dress who's working behind the counter. "Oh, Lulu! We have a doubter. Can you bring us one of your fabulous eggnog hot cocoas to try?"

"Coming right up. Followed by one eggnog hot cocoa convert."

Quinn rubs her hands together. "I. Can't. Wait."

I narrow my eyes. "You planned all along to sneak the eggnog in, didn't you?"

"Of course I did. I'm a planner," she says with a wink as Lulu swings by, setting down a ceramic cup with panache.

"I dare you not to fall in love," Lulu declares.

I glance between them suspiciously. "Ladies, why do I feel like you know something I don't?"

Quinn points excitedly to the cup. "Try it. Lulu is a goddess of all things chocolate, and she can convert even the most skeptical. Like you."

I bring the concoction to my lips, and it's . . . rich and creamy and chocolaty and tastes like nutmeg and Christmas mornings and promises. I don't even try to hide my satisfied grin. "It tastes like the best present ever feels."

Quinn shimmies her arms in victory. "Knew it, called it. Pay up."

"And split it with me," Lulu says as she returns behind the counter.

I offer the cup to Quinn. "Let's see how it tastes on your lips."

"Yes. Let's do that." Her eyes glitter as she takes a sip. When she sets down the cup, she lifts her chin —an offering. I groan quietly as I slide my hand through her soft locks and brush my lips over hers. She murmurs as I kiss her, melting into our embrace.

I taste the chocolate, the nutmeg, and the sweetness of her.

My mind crackles, humming with electricity even when I break the kiss at last. "Tastes even better."

She's inches away, her eyes locked with mine. "But you should try again just to be sure."

"That is a brilliant idea." I bring her close for one more kiss. As my lips slide over hers, I'm sure this is the best time I've had with a woman in ages. I'm certain, too, that I like this woman even more than I did last night.

I suppose that means I'm falling further.

I need to make the most of the time we have before the cutoff date and our clean, harmless ending.

"Quinn," I say, pulling apart from her as I brush the back of my fingers along her cheek. "Since I know you like a heads-up, I'm going to ask you to come home with me tonight. And once you're there, I want to make sure you stay on the naughty list for a very long time."

She grabs her purse, her hat, and her coat. "Check, please."

\* \* \*

The trek to my home is like foreplay.

We leave holding hands.

In the cab, I kiss her neck, savoring the vanilla-honey scent of her hair, the fresh smell of her skin. I flick my tongue over the shell of her ear.

"If you do that again, I might jump you here in the back seat, and that would be rude," she murmurs.

"I'd hate for us to be rude," I whisper, but then I nibble on her earlobe for good measure.

"You were warned," she says as she slides a hand up my thigh.

"Well, I'm not sure I want to heed your warnings if that's where they go."

She laughs, and I do too, and then we behave till we reach my building.

All bets are off in the elevator though.

As soon as the doors close, I clasp her face and kiss her hard.

Like I've wanted to all along—hard and passionate, with everything I have. She lifts her chin, loops her arms around my neck, and asks for more, not with words, but with the way she arches against me, with how she plays with the ends of my hair.

We reach my floor, and the walk to the end of the hall is interminable, so I lift her, toss her over my shoulder, and carry her, picking up the pace.

She pounds playfully against my back with her fists. "Hey, I'm not that slow."

"I know. But I'm really fast," I say, reaching the door in seconds and setting her down.

But I can't resist one more kiss. I lean in, draw her close, and seal my mouth to hers as I reach for the keys in my pocket. She tastes so damn good, and all I want is to have more of her. To experience all of her.

To learn all the flavors of Quinn.

And with that heady possibility luring me, I open the door.

As soon as it snicks shut, she smiles at me.

And hell, it does me in, like it has since the night I met her.

Tonight, it's a new kind of smile. A sexy, sensual one. A delicious, inviting grin.

Our coats come off, and she reaches for the collar of my shirt, tugs me close once more, and whispers three fantastic words. "I want you."

Then she adds two more to make it even more perfect. "So much."

I groan and wrap her in my arms. "Spoiler alert—the feeling is mutual."

She laughs, and I do too, and like that, a new round of kissing takes us all the way to the bedroom.

# 11

## QUINN

It's been a year.

Twelve months without someone's touch, without contact.

But that's not why I'm buzzing with anticipation. That's not why my skin sizzles with every brush of his hands, every sweep of his lips.

The way I feel has everything to do with chemistry —*our* chemistry—and the way he looks at me, touches me, treats me.

That one most of all.

I've only known him a short while, but he treats me like I'm precious.

And he touches me the same way.

He sets me on the edge of his bed, unzips my boots, and runs his big hands up my calves.

My smooth, shaven legs.

He touches me reverently, and it's addictive. It makes me shudder.

His hands play with the hem of my skirt, then my

sweater, his dark eyes glinting. He lifts it over my head, and I help him along, taking off my cami next, and my skirt too.

Then I'm in only a red lace bra with white stripes and matching panties. His eyes widen as he takes in my lingerie.

"Merry Christmas to me, and it's not even Thanksgiving," he says, his voice smoky.

I give him a naughty grin. "I thought you might like the holiday decor. Since you do seem to enjoy Christmas decorations."

Running his fingers over the lacy material of my bra, he asks, "And is this what we'd call a candy cane cocktail?"

I shake my head, letting my gaze drift down his long, tall frame, settling on the zipper of his jeans, a grin playing on my lips. "No, but I'm hoping that is."

He shakes his head. "Such a dirty girl."

Then he kicks off his shoes, flops on the bed next to me, and pulls me over so I'm straddling him. His hands rise, threading through my hair, and he brings me down for another kiss.

Only this one is hotter.

Deeper.

Fevered.

It's a prelude to the rest of the night.

The trouble is . . .

I break the kiss. "You're still dressed."

He looks down at his Henley as if shocked. "Yeah, what's up with that? Why aren't you getting me naked, woman?"

I press my hands to his chest and shoot him a saucy look. "Because you keep kissing me and distracting me, that's why."

"Well, I'm distraction-free right now," he says, and waits patiently.

But I don't make him wait long. I make quick work of his shirt, marveling at his broad chest and tracing my fingers over his firm pecs, his toned arms.

Even though he's no longer playing, the man has an athlete's body, and he's not just *firm*. He's rock-hard, with strong muscles and carved abs. He's fantastic to touch.

We shift around, and I unbutton his jeans. Then he kicks them off the rest of the way, and I draw a sharp breath when I see the outline in his boxer briefs.

"Maybe I've been a very good girl after all," I murmur in appreciation.

"Is that so?"

I reach out, pressing a hand to his erection. His eyes shut, and he groans as I stroke him.

I don't need a man to be huge. I don't have visions of giant sugarplum cocks dancing in my head.

But I don't have to peek inside Vaughn's pants to know I like this present. I like it a lot.

I remove his briefs, biting my lip as I stroke him. "This is the kind of surprise I enjoy."

He chuckles. "Glad I could deliver for you."

"Did I say you'd delivered yet?" I tease him.

His eyes snap open, and in a flash, he flips me to my back, pins my wrists, and stares hotly at me. "And for that, you're going to get extra special attention."

"You were planning to hold back before?"

His eyes narrow. "You were always getting the full treatment. But now I think you need extra orgasms for that sassy attitude."

"I can be sassier. I can bring the sarcasm if it brings me Os."

"And Os I will deliver." Then he silences me with a kiss—a deep, sweet kiss that makes my toes curl. Moving down my body, he strips me as he goes, taking off my bra and lavishing attention on my breasts, making me moan as I curl my hands in his hair.

Then he makes me gasp and cry out when he slides off my panties, spreads my legs, and kisses me where I'm aching for him.

My hips shoot off the bed, and I'm already saying his name.

It's that good.

He's that attentive.

He seems to revel in licking me, tasting me. In *having* me like dessert. Because that's how he goes down on me—as if I'm the sweetest thing he's had in ages. His tongue is magic. His lips send sparks of pleasure all over my body. I grab at the sheets. I grab at his hair. I moan and groan in bliss.

"So good," he murmurs as he consumes me. "You taste so fucking good, Quinn."

His words, the way he growls them—that's all I need.

Desire coils in me, tightening, and then I'm calling out his name as pleasure obliterates my senses and I'm nothing but white-hot bliss.

Seconds later, he crawls over me, his lips hooked in a crooked grin. "You were saying?"

I grin. Wickedly. "Let's see if I'm clear on how this works. If I sass you again, I get more orgasms?"

"Sure," he replies. "Think of it as a special delivery."

"I do like extra presents."

Laughing, he rolls his eyes. "Quinn Summers, you are absolutely fucking awesome in every way."

I beam, the gleam coming from deep inside my chest. *This man.* He just does it for me. "Well, let's see if the fucking is awesome," I toss back.

With a smile, he stretches his arm to the nightstand, reaching for a condom, I presume.

But something he said last night sticks with me. *I've been all about work since then. And I'm better off without her.* "Vaughn . . ."

"Yeah?"

"I haven't been with anyone in a year. I'm clean, and I'm on protection."

His lips curve up. "I've been a monk too, and I'm safe."

He drops the condom back into the drawer, moves over me, and lifts my arms above my head. I tremble.

The feel of him is extraordinary. The weight of him. The *heat.*

I cup his cheek. "I need you to know, this doesn't feel like just sex," I whisper.

With that, I surprise myself.

Because I was wrong.

Wrong about being safe from hurt.

Wrong about being impervious to heartache.

And I was dead wrong to think that ending this will be easy.

My heart's already onboard. It will ache when he leaves.

But tonight is about feeling good.

And I feel amazing when he answers me with "I need you to know it won't be just sex for me."

My heart melts a little more.

Settling between my thighs, he guides himself into me, and I moan instantly, my eyes floating closed. I've been so turned on all night, and now I finally have him, this man I desperately want. This man who knows what to do with me.

He takes his time till he's all the way in, and I gasp once he's there. The feeling is extraordinary. My bones hum, and tingles race down my spine.

I widen my legs and wrap my arms around his neck, craving closeness.

He takes his time, listening to my cues, finding a rhythm. Soon, we're moving like we know each other's bodies. Like we were meant to be tangled up together.

He raises up on his arms, reaching for my right leg and hooking me tighter around him. At that angle, he goes deeper, and I nearly lose my mind with pleasure.

"Oh God," I pant, then I look up at him, meeting his eyes. They're so intense right now. I swear I see something in them. Something I haven't seen before.

And that look, it makes me want to connect with him. He slows our pace, tantalizing me with unhurried thrusts. "Hi," I whisper, wanting, hoping he feels the same thrilling new thing I do. This wild beating in my heart.

"Hi to you." His voice tells me he does. His voice and the way he talks to me, the way he looks at me.

"This feels incredible," I whisper.

"Yeah. There's no other word for it."

Soon we speed up, a pace that sends pulse after pulse of pleasure through me.

I'm getting closer to the edge. So damn close. I'll be there any second. He swivels his hips and drives into me, making me unleash a string of *oh God, oh Gods*.

He moves faster, rocking harder, groaning too.

My hands grip him tighter. I need the connection. I feel it so deeply already as my stomach flutters and pleasure races through me, hard and fast, sending me over once more.

I call his name, and the world spirals away as he follows me, joining me on the other side.

His smile is devilish as he grins at me, so satisfied. "You were saying?"

I laugh and run a hand through his hair. "I was saying . . . I'll keep sassing you."

"You do that."

He excuses himself to go to the restroom and returns a few seconds later with a warm washcloth, running it gently between my legs. His tenderness makes my chest ache, my throat tighten.

Part of me wishes this was just sex.

But I can't go back.

It's so much more for me, and for him.

That's the biggest surprise of the night, and I don't know how to deal with it.

But before I decide anything, I need to know the score.

# 12

## VAUGHN

"Spend the night." I run my hand along her waist as I make my request, savoring the feel of her.

"Does that mean I'm still on the naughty list?" she asks, a little playful, a little coy.

"You're on the I-want-to-wake-up-next-to-you list," I say.

As soon as I voice it, her expression shifts. Gone is the sass, and in its place is something else—something vulnerable. "I want to be on that list."

"You definitely are."

She props herself on her elbow, resting her head in her hand. "At the risk of being totally forward, but also admitting I love to know what's going on . . ." She takes a deep, bracing breath. "What are we doing?"

Part of me wants to play it cool. Keep it casual. Act like this is no big deal.

A bigger part of me wants to confess she's doing things to me I never expected.

Or maybe I did. Didn't I say the night I met her that

Quinn was my tailor-made temptation? That she could be the one to make me break my fast?

I knew the first time I talked to her—knew deep inside—we'd wind up here. Not just in bed, but in bed connecting.

In bed wanting more.

I want as much of her as I can have, and I don't need to hide that.

"What are we doing?" I wiggle my brow because I can't resist teasing her. "I think we're doing each other." Then I bring her close and wrap my arms around her. "But I also think we should keep doing it. Keep seeing each other. Keep spending time together. What do you think?"

Nerves crawl up my chest as I wait for her answer.

She takes a beat, then nods. "I think that sounds like an excellent plan."

"Also, I should probably give your brother a heads-up. Since it's the right thing to do. Are you cool with that?"

She laughs. "Let's tell him now," she says, grabbing her phone. "Group chat?"

I shrug happily. "Let's do it." I search for my phone while she taps out a text then sends it. He replies before I can even unlock my screen.

**Quinn:** Hi. Vaughn is hot and sweet and awesome. I'm going to date him. If you were Amy, I'd think you planned it, with all those phone calls you took at dinner when I met him, but since you're you, I know it was accidental. So, thanks for hating parties.

**Josh:** You're right. I don't have a matchmaking bone in my body. And you're always welcome for the party hatred. Also, good choice in men.

**Vaughn:** Aren't we all so adult and mature. Everyone deserves a gold star.

Quinn and I toss our phones onto the pillow, and she grins at me. "Told you."

I kiss her nose. Then pull back to look at her. "So does that mean you're mine for the holidays?"

"I'm yours."

"Good, then I'd really like to have you again."

And I do, that night then in the morning too.

And we make plans.

Plans make her happy. They make me happy too, because they mean I'm going to see her.

A lot of her.

Like a few nights later.

We walk up Fifth Avenue after dinner, checking out store displays and talking about family. I tell her about Callie and Danny and how excited I am to see them over Thanksgiving and then on a more regular basis when I live in Miami.

"That's great that you'll get to see them so frequently," she says. "I don't know what I'd do if I couldn't see Amy whenever I wanted to. You should meet her."

My heart thumps a little harder, thrilled that she brought it up. I squeeze her hand. "I'd love to."

We go to her place that night, where we test out the strength of her kitchen counter.

"I can feel you so far in me," she says, gasping.

She loves it when I hook her legs around my waist. When I take her deep. When I bring her down hard on me.

"That. When you do that," she moans.

"I'll do whatever you need, whatever you want to get you there."

"You. I want you."

She loves it, too, when I thread my hand through her hair and kiss her neck as I bring her to the edge of the cliff.

She seems to hover there, gasping, panting, moaning. God, she's so fucking sexy, so incredibly gorgeous when she falls apart in my arms. When I follow her there, my body feels electric, pleasure pulsing in me.

My heart races. It could be from the exertion, but when she clasps my face and pulls me close, I'm pretty sure it's from something more. "It's sooo not sex at all," she whispers.

"I know, Quinn. I know."

* * *

The next night, we visit an arcade that rents Skee-Ball machines for parties, and she places an order for the holiday bash.

Then we return to my apartment again.

In the elevator, I run into the head of the co-op board, who beams and launches right into chatter. "Everything is going swimmingly with the offer on your place."

"That's great news," I say, and Quinn looks away as the woman and I chat.

Hell, there's a part of me that wants to look away, too, from what's coming at the end of the year.

But we both know the score.

We knew from the start.

When we reach my apartment, Quinn offers a smile. "Looks like your place was an easy sale," she says.

"It should be off my hands pretty soon."

"And you have a place in Miami already?" Her voice is the slightest bit strained.

"I made an offer a few days ago."

"You're going to be so happy there," she says. Then she presses her lips to mine, and I feel happy right here too.

And that's exactly the problem.

# 13

## QUINN

It's official. I'm going to burst.

I point accusingly at my sister. "Why did you let me do this?"

Josh chimes in. "You do this every year."

"It's because Mom makes the best stuffing. And mashed potatoes. And green bean casserole."

Mom raises her hand, owning it. "I do. It's all true. And your father is a champion turkey carver."

"I'm the best, and none of you kids can resist my birds," he says.

*Kids.* I look around at my thirty-six-year-old brother and his fiancée. At my older sister, Tabitha, who flew home from Paris for the holiday, and at Amy.

I adore them all madly, and I'm so glad they're here. We're hardly children anymore, but I love that my dad still calls us "kids." I love that I can see them often like this, as a family.

Except for Tabitha. "Tab, when are you going to move back here? We miss you."

She waves a hand airily. "Someday. I miss you all too."

"We demand to see more of you," Amy says, banging a fist on the table. "I see this stinker almost every week." She points at me.

"I second that demand," I say with a laugh, then I toss my napkin on the table. "After all, don't you miss Amy's baked goods? She brought me peanut butter cookies earlier this week, and they were divine."

"Speaking of my divine baking," Amy says, shooting me a stern stare, "you better have saved room for my world-famous walnut pie."

"As if I didn't," I say.

Tabitha pats her belly. "My dessert compartment is open for business."

As Amy serves the slices of pie, a wave of contentment washes over me. I'm happy here. Delightfully so.

The only thing that would make this better would be if Vaughn were here too.

And because there's no reason to hold back, I tell him that night via text.

**Quinn:** Thanksgiving was amazing, but I have a confession.

**Vaughn:** You ate all the leftovers already? Oh wait, that was me.

**Quinn:** You are going to be in so much trouble. But that's not my confession.

**Vaughn:** Don't make a man wait. Especially since I have one for you too.

**Quinn:** Ooh, what's yours?

**Vaughn:** I miss you like crazy.

**Quinn:** Same. I miss you so much. I'm counting down till I see you again. It's four miserable days.

**Vaughn:** Four endless days.

**Quinn:** Four lonely nights.

**Vaughn:** Stop, or I'm going to fly back early, and I can't do that. But I want to. Badly.

**Quinn:** Just know the sex will be red-hot when you return—I want you that much.

**Vaughn:** And I'm on the next plane.

He doesn't catch the next flight, but when I see him the Sunday after Thanksgiving, all systems are go.

I fling open the door, yank him in by the collar, and strip off his shirt in seconds flat.

"You did miss me," he muses.

"I miss you, I want you, I need you. Now get inside me."

He laughs, scoops me up, and carries me to my bed. "Inside you is the only place I want to be."

Before I know it, I'm naked on all fours, and he's banding an arm around my waist and fucking me hard.

It's delicious and dirty, rough and frenzied. It's everything I want from him. And the orgasm is so intense, my entire body shakes, and the sounds I make are animalistic.

As I'm coming down, he flips me over so I'm on my back, then hooks my legs around him. "Want to look at you. Want to see your face."

He stares at me intently, the vein in his neck pulsing as he thrusts deeper—so deep I see stars.

The pleasure is almost too much.

But I'm feeling more than pleasure.

When I fall over the edge again, I'm falling into him.

Into a love I shouldn't let myself feel.

Later, when we're half-dressed, he does the very thing he promised to do the night we met.

He doesn't need a step stool or a crate. He simply raises a strong arm and sets a glittery red star on the top of the tree.

"I believe this was your fantasy." There's a gleam in his eye, a knowing sort of look. "How's reality living up to it?"

I tap my chin, surveying the living room and the windows that show off the first flakes of falling snow.

"Hmm. If memory serves, I didn't tell you the rest of the fantasy I had that night."

He closes the distance, loops an arm around my waist, and tugs me closer. "Tell me now."

"Well, it involves you decorating all the tallest branches, stringing the lights, and, pretty please, hanging up all the Christmas decorations in the rest of my apartment."

He growls at me. "Not what I was hoping to hear."

"Oh, wait. I forgot something." I stand on tiptoe and whisper in his ear.

And boy, does that man make fast work of the decorating so we can turn off all the lights save the blinking ones on the tree.

Nat King Cole plays softly from the speakers as Vaughn brings me to the couch and makes love to me while the snow falls and blue-and-white bulbs wink on and off.

What can I say? This woman has Christmas sex fantasies, and this man is fulfilling them.

Every. Single. One.

Including the classic snow-day fantasy.

We wake up to twelve inches that drifted down overnight.

Yes, I make jokes about twelve inches.

But mostly we hunker down together. The city is nearly shut down, so we both work from home, making calls, answering emails, and then ignoring calls and emails because being naked is so much more fun.

"Best snow day ever," he says that night in the shower.

"Yes, and you've worn me out so much I need a day off tomorrow," I say, teasing him.

"Sorry, not sorry."

That night, we slide under the covers, and he draws his fingertips down my shoulder, kissing me as he goes. "Quinn...?"

"Yes?"

He props himself up on his elbow, looking at me. "Have I ever told you about the time I broke my diet in a truly spectacular fashion?"

I laugh. "I didn't realize you were on one."

He slashes a hand through the air. "Total woman fast. Complete romance-free diet. I was zero women, zero dates, zero romance."

"You're hard-core."

He nods exaggeratedly. "All the way. All or nothing. I was on the nothing side for the last year. And now..."

My chest warms. "And now?"

His eyes lock with mine. "I'm on the *all* side."

My whole body is glowing, lit from head to toe with so many bright and powerful emotions. "I'm on the same side."

It's blissful and painful to spend another night in his arms, wishing I could make the next month last forever.

Of course, I can't. And perhaps that's why I feel free to tell him what's going on in my heart. Maybe that's the unexpected benefit of an expiration date—you can be more honest with nothing to lose.

"Hey, you," I whisper when I turn off the lights.

"Hey to you too."

"Did you know I'm going to miss you when you leave?"

His smile is a bit sad. "Tell me about it. I'm going to miss you like crazy. How the hell did that happen?"

I frown, punching him playfully. "Exactly. You're not supposed to be so likable."

"I could say the same about you being all funny and sweet and too good to be true. You really ought to cut it out."

I laugh, but it's tinged with wistfulness too. "And you. Please stop being wonderful."

He shakes his head. "Nope. I promise I won't stop treating you like you're the one person I want to spend every night with."

My heart aches, knowing those nights are winding down far too soon.

In the morning, I say goodbye as he heads to the office, then I make my way to the shower so I can do the same. The next two weeks pass in a blur of falling snow, final party prep, and all our December nights and mornings together.

The evening of the fete, as I shower and get ready to meet Vaughn, something hits me.

Something I've been missing.

Something that is *three days late*.

# 14

## VAUGHN

"Whoa."

That's the reaction from Callie when I show her my nearly empty apartment on FaceTime.

"And this surprises you?" I ask.

She shakes her head, then nods. "Yes. No. I mean, it doesn't surprise me, because I've got all the boxes here at your new condo," she says, panning around to show me the place in Florida, stacked with the boxes I shipped down, plus most of my furniture. "But it does raise the question—where are you sleeping?"

A grin threatens to take over my face, but I school my expression. "Quinn's."

One brow arches. "Every night?"

I count off quietly, stopping when I'm well past ten. "Yeah, every night, I guess."

"Huh."

"What's the 'huh' for?"

"The 'huh' stands for 'What are you going to do when you can't see her every night?'"

I hate the thought of not seeing her. And I hate hating, so I do my best to avoid the pain of the question. "Then I won't see her," I say as matter-of-factly as I can.

"And how do you feel about that?"

I give her a look like her question doesn't compute. "Did you wake up in the body of Freud this morning? 'And how does that make you feel?'" I ask, mimicking her.

*Wow. That came out kind of snotty.*

"And I have my answer," she says.

I drag my free hand through my hair. "Sorry. I didn't mean to act like an ass. To answer your question—it sucks. That's how I feel. But what can I do?"

She grins like she knows something I don't. "Oh, gee. I don't know."

"Callie," I huff.

She rolls her eyes. "Do you want me to spell it out?"

"Sure."

"Keep. Seeing. Her."

"Long-distance?" I ask, as if she's just suggested Quinn and I commute to Mars every weekend.

"Yes. Long-distance. Why not? It's only a two-and-a-half-hour flight. You have the money."

"Yeah, but . . ."

"But what's the 'but'?"

I scrub my hand over my jaw, trying to figure that out. Is there a "but" anymore? Quinn and I have spent the last month together, four intense weeks where we can't seem to get enough of each other, like we're trying to inhale all the goodness before it's gone.

And it's all been good.

Every damn second with her has been great.

Like I said to Quinn, I'm an all-or-nothing guy. I've given her my all. I *feel* all in. Once I'd experienced a taste of her, I couldn't stop.

The last thing I want from Quinn is the "nothing" part. Not after we've had the "all."

Which brings me to Callie's question.

"But I was trying to avoid romantic entanglements," I point out.

She laughs like that's the funniest thing anyone's ever said. "How's that working out for you?"

I laugh, too, at the bluntness of her question. At the awareness I have now that I didn't a month ago. And at the chance that's now in front of me. I broke my no-romance rule in a spectacular fashion, and I want to keep on breaking it. I want to find a way with Quinn.

Screw expiration dates. Callie's right—I should ask Quinn if she wants to stay together.

"It's working out great," I say dryly.

"Yeah, you're doing a top-notch job at being single."

I blow out a long stream of air. "I just ask her to do the long-distance thing? It's that simple?"

Callie smiles, bright and excited. "What's the worst that can happen? She says no, and then you do what you'd planned anyway—which is *not* see her."

The worst thing that could happen sounds pretty damned bad.

And so, I can't let it. I need to do more than ask her to stay together.

I need to tell her the one thing I haven't yet. The thing I've been keeping inside.

I have to let her know that I'm already madly in love with her and I don't ever want to let her go.

## 15

# QUINN

I. Can't. Breathe.

My stomach is upside down.

My world is inside out.

Amy guides me from my bathroom to the couch in my apartment, draping an arm around me.

"How did this happen?" I ask, my voice stretched thin.

"Well, when a man loves a woman—"

"I know how it happened! But how the hell did it happen?"

She shrugs, rubbing my shoulder. "Protection doesn't always work perfectly. I guess you're in the one percent of something." I drop my head into my hands, breathing hard. She runs her hand over my back. "It's going to be okay."

I snap my head up. "How?" I cry out. "How is it going to be okay? The father of my child is leaving. I'm going to be a thirty-year-old single mom."

She flashes me a cheery smile. "You're going to be

an *awesome* thirty-year-old single mom. And your baby is going to have an amazing aunt, because I am going to be here for you. So will Josh and Mom and Dad, and maybe even Tabitha when she deigns to return from Paris. But that's beside the point. You're going to be all right. That's what matters."

I gulp, emotion clogging my throat, tears filling my eyes. "I love babies. I love kids. I want them. I just didn't expect to have one accidentally. When I'm not even married. Or engaged. Or living with the father. I'm not even *with* him," I say, my voice breaking.

Amy waggles her head in a *maybe, maybe not* way, saying softly, "Well, you kind of are."

"But I'm not. *We're* not."

"You've spent the last month hunkered down in your apartment watching Netflix Christmas specials and banging to 'Rockin' Around the Christmas Tree.'"

I laugh at her summary of my relationship with Vaughn. "I wouldn't say we did much watching of Christmas specials."

She stares pointedly at my belly. "That much is apparent. And so is my point—you two pretty much are together."

The pang in my heart returns, the ache that happens every time I think about him leaving. But I try to focus on the practical. "We agreed it would end when he moves. That was always the plan. But *this*? This, I did not plan."

A laugh bubbles from Amy's chest. "That's the part that's hard for you, isn't it? Since you hate surprises so much."

"They're the worst. But what if it was a mistake? Should I take another test?" I ask, voice wobbling.

"Sure. If you think the five you already took were wrong."

I wince, squeezing my eyes shut. "Ames . . ."

"Quinn," she says, soft but firm. "You're going to be an amazing mom."

I let her words sink in, let the reality wash over me. *I'm going to be a mother. I'm going to have a baby.*

It's all so thoroughly unexpected, and I have no clue what to do with surprises.

But I know this: I have to be at the party in thirty minutes.

I take a deep breath, wipe away my tears, and put on my best party-planner face.

Because in thirty minutes, I'm going to see the man who's walking out of my life while I'm carrying a piece of him inside me.

And I'm going to have to deliver one hell of a surprise.

## 16

## QUINN

*Just do it.*

*Just tell him when you see him.*

*Just say the words.*

I repeat these new mantras as I head to the boutique hotel.

As I walk through the entryway, I flash back to the night we first visited this place, and a smile tugs at my lips as I recall how we clicked. How he found the mistletoe in the hallway and gave me a heads-up before he swept me away with a kiss.

A kiss that made me swoon.

A kiss that melted me from head to toe.

He still kisses me that way. He kisses me with passion and tenderness, with hunger and need. And lately, with something more.

My heart flutters, and I set a hand on my chest as I walk into the lobby, thinking of how it feels when Vaughn kisses me now. It feels like he wants all the same things I do.

*All of them?*

A woman can hope.

My hand slides to my belly.

It's flat now, but if all goes well, it won't be flat for long.

And even though I didn't plan for this change in my life, I can prep every damn day for the next nine months. Even though babies have a way of surprising you, I can handle this. I can do it on my own if I have to, because I know how to do things. I'll make a plan.

And as "Have Yourself a Merry Little Christmas" floats through the lobby, sparkling with white flickering lights and decorated with wreaths, I don't feel sad.

Which is odd because this song brings out the loneliest parts of me. The hurt parts of me. But as I listen to it now, I don't feel that pain I used to. I don't feel the sadness in my bones.

I feel . . . possibility.

I feel hope for the life inside me.

And I feel certain that even though I *can* do this alone, I don't want to.

I want Vaughn beside me.

*The man I love.*

I have more to tell him than the baby news. I plan to tell him that I'm in love with him too, no matter how scary that is.

I want it all, and I want it all with him.

I take a deep breath and head into the venue. I'm the first one here because it's my job to be early and check, then make sure, that everything is in place.

The tree looks magical, lit up and decorated with

red-and-white bows and sporty ornaments—footballs and basketballs and baseballs and more, all with the names of Premiere's clients on them. Garlands festoon the walls. A Skee-Ball machine occupies one corner. In another, a hot chocolate bar is ready to go. The catering staff has prepped yummy appetizers and a full buffet. Athletes have big appetites, after all.

Everything is ready.

And I suppose I need to be ready too.

We likely won't have a minute alone till late into the night, so I'll tell him everything when the party ends.

*Deep breath.*

I square my shoulders as the music switches to "Frosty the Snowman." The memory of how we shared this song makes me laugh.

Then it makes me tingle.

*Oh.*

That's not a memory. That's a finger brushing down my spine. A hand lifting the hair from my neck. Lips pressing gently to my skin.

And a voice in my ear. "Just to let you know, I'm madly in love with you, Quinn."

I spin around and meet the eyes of the man I've fallen for. All my plans for the night fly out the window.

"I'm pregnant."

## 17

## VAUGHN

That wasn't on my radar at all.

Not anywhere on the list of possibilities I entertained when I walked in early for the party, expecting she'd be here but never expecting her to tell me *that*.

I figured if I was lucky, she'd say she was in love with me too.

If I was really lucky, she'd want to stay together.

And if I was really fucking lucky, she'd tell me she'd move to Florida with me.

But that's not what she's saying.

She's having a baby. *Our baby.*

"You are?" I ask, my head swimming with news I didn't see coming in a million Christmases.

"Yes. And I'm sure that's a shock, since I was on protection, and I don't know why it didn't work. I took the pill religiously every morning at six a.m. I even have an alarm set. I've never ever missed a day, and that's why I took five tests. I wanted to take one more, but Amy felt five was enough," she blurts out.

"Amy knows?" I ask, processing this bombshell.

She nods speedily. "I couldn't take them alone, and I didn't want to freak you out. I needed someone, so she came over with another pack. I'd already bought two. She knew I'd want more."

A smile tugs at my lips. I'd have predicted five too. "Of course you'd want to be sure. That's who you are."

"You know me so well," she says, and it's an offhand comment, but entirely true. She breathes out hard, continuing, "And all five had two pink lines."

"Wow," I say, taking it all in.

Taking *her* in. The vulnerability in her eyes. The worry in her face. The honesty in her words.

But most of all, I see what I've always seen.

*My future.*

There are no questions, no buts. The "nothing" option is off the table, and now it's time to have it all.

I set a hand on her belly, drawing a deep breath. "So we're having a baby?"

Her eyes widen to moon pies. "What?"

A smile takes over my face. "Well, I'm presuming that's your plan, Miss Woman with a Plan? *We're* going to have the baby, right?"

"We?" She squeaks like Minnie Mouse.

Wait.

Did I read this wrong? Read *her* wrong? I step back, regarding her curiously. "Do you want to have the baby by yourself?"

She gestures wildly to me. "Do you want to have the baby with me?" Her voice is so high it hits the ceiling.

I laugh like she's crazy. "I just told you I'm in love with you. I was hoping you felt the same way about me."

"Yes!" Her shout reaches an octave I didn't know existed. "But . . . but . . . also, I should have said that first. Yes, I'm in love with you. I just—"

"You're just surprised."

Her eyes are soft and brimming with happiness. "Yes."

"But are you surprised I'm in love with you? I was kind of hoping it had been obvious."

"I like obvious. And I'm happy about that. Wildly happy." She swipes away a tear streaking down her cheek as her voice returns to normal and she takes some deep breaths. "I'm so in love with you too. But I didn't think—"

"That I'd want to have a baby with you?" I ask quizzically.

"I don't want you to think you have to stay with me because of the baby," she says.

I wrap my arm around her, bringing her close and sliding my hand over her belly again. "I don't have to. I want to. I came here early to tell you there's no way I'm letting you go. I was going to ask you to stay with me. That was my plan tonight. See? I had a plan. Your favorite thing."

She smiles like she can't contain her grin. "I do like plans. I like that *that* was your plan."

"I wanted to find a way to keep you, even before I knew you were pregnant, because I love you, Quinn Summers. And guess what? I still love you, and I still want to be with you. And—spoiler alert—I'm going to love our baby too." I take a moment to look into her eyes. "So, are we doing this?"

She melts against me. "Yes. But this kind of changes everything, doesn't it?"

I laugh, tuck a finger under her chin, and answer her. "Yes, it changes literally everything. And I know you were diligent about taking the pill—I heard your alarm every morning. But this is a good surprise. Some surprises are great surprises."

Her smile radiates into my soul. "I'm glad you feel that way." She lets out a long breath. "So, what do we do?"

I don't have the answer yet, and I'm not going to try to find it just now, because my business partners are strolling into the room. With Quinn's hand in mine, I head over to join them.

Later, we'll figure out what this means. Tonight, we have a party to throw. And when the guests stream in, I pull Quinn close and murmur a reminder to only drink the unspiked hot chocolate—not because she needs me to tell her, but because it makes her smile, like we have a secret. And we do.

It's a secret I'm in love with already.

# 18

## VAUGHN

There are plans. There are damn plans. And there are babies. When the party ends, I take Quinn back to her place.

She plugs in the lights for the tree, turns on a playlist on her phone, and tugs me by the hand to her couch.

"So . . ."

"So, is there something you wanted to talk about?" I tease.

She swats me. "Yes. Only, say, *everything*."

I settle into the couch and fold my hands. "We're going to be here a long time then, if we're talking about everything. Where should we start? How dinosaurs became extinct? The ancient Roman aqueducts? Are eyebrows considered facial hair?"

She shoots me a look. "Don't mess with the pregnant woman."

I lean back against the couch, enjoying myself. "Are you going to use that on me for the next nine months?"

She strokes her chin. "Hmm . . . Yes. Yes, I am." She takes a deep breath, turning serious again. "What are we doing?"

I run the backs of my fingers down her cheek and give her the simplest and truest answer. "We're having a baby."

She swallows, and it looks like it hurts. "But you're moving."

"Yeah, about that."

Her shoulders tense, and I hate that she's worried. I can't let her think I'd leave her for even a second.

I sit up straight and meet her gaze. "Quinn, I can't ask you to move when you're pregnant. I can't ask you to leave your family and your sister. Not when you need them now more than ever."

Her lips part, and she seems poised and on edge. "You can't?"

I shake my head. "No. So there's only one solution."

"What's that?"

I glance around at her place and sigh heavily. "I sold my home. I'm going to need a place to stay in Manhattan."

"To stay?" Her pitch hits another octave again.

I slide my hand through her hair. "Let me give you a heads-up. If you ask me to move in with you, I'm going to say yes."

She squeals. "But what about Miami? And the firm's expansion plans? And the condo you bought?"

I grin. Wickedly. "I might have a surprise for you."

"What is it? I hate surprises."

"Oh, you'll like this one."

"I will?"

"I talked to my business partners tonight. Don't worry—I didn't tell them your news. *Our* news," I correct. "But I asked how they'd feel if we didn't expand just yet."

"What did they say?"

"They're fine with it. It was an expansion after all, not a necessity. And look, I may need to travel to Florida. But the reality is there are four of us. We'll take turns. We're a partnership. So we'll table the expansion plans for now. Besides," I say, my hand straying to her belly again, "life threw us a surprise, and it seems these other expansion plans are going to have to take precedence."

She climbs onto my lap, glee in her green eyes. Clasping my face, she looks at me, holding my gaze. "Will you move in with me? Tonight?"

"Yes. Yes, I will."

I pull her close and seal our vow with a kiss. A kiss that soon turns heated. In fact, it's so hot that in no time we're reenacting what got us here in the first place.

# EPILOGUE

*Quinn*

When I wake up on Christmas Day, New York City has given me a gift—a fresh blanket of snow.

I draw a deep breath, savoring the morning as I head to the window and drink in the sight. White. Everywhere I see white, and it's magical.

My man gives me a gift too—a mug of eggnog hot chocolate.

Unspiked, of course.

"Merry Christmas, Quinn," he says when I join him in the living room at the tree.

"Merry Christmas, Vaughn," I say, a little giddy because I still can't believe this is my life. That he's in it when he was supposed to be out of it. That a little something unexpected gave me everything I don't want to live without.

And I can't wait for him to open his present. I head

to the tree and grab it, then hand him the red-wrapped box.

He holds it up, shakes it. "Quinn, I know it's the pony I asked for. I peeked last night."

"Oh, stop. Just open it."

He unwraps the gift and smiles when he holds up a T-shirt with a *T* logo like we joked about the night we met. "Just a little something to remind you that you were my Christmas fantasy."

He loops an arm around my waist and tugs me onto his lap, peppering me with kisses—my ears, my neck, my lips.

He dotes on me, and I'm only six weeks pregnant. I can only imagine what the rest of my life will be like with him.

*Wonderful.*

They'll be wonderful years.

"Thank you," he murmurs, then his dark eyes gleam. "I got you something too."

I glance at the tree. It's empty underneath. "I don't see a gift," I say, playfully chiding him.

"Because I know you so well. I would never leave your gift under the tree. You confessed your dirty little secret the first night we met."

I pout. "But I love Christmas and Christmas presents. And you. I love you."

"Good," he says, sliding me off him then dropping to one knee. "Then I hope you don't need a heads-up that I'm about to ask you to marry me."

I gasp, and a nanosecond later, tears slide down my cheeks.

He meets my gaze. "I fell in love with you the night we met, and I love you more every day. And I love our baby. Let's be a family. Will you marry me?"

"Yes! I'd hoped you were going to ask."

He slides the ring onto my finger and brings me in for a delicious Christmas-morning kiss.

When we separate, I look into his eyes. "This is the best present ever."

We don't wait long to tie the knot. About six weeks later on Valentine's Day, we get married in a small wedding with family and close friends in attendance.

We spend the next several months living and loving, getting our apartment ready, selling his condo in Miami, and flying to Florida every month to see his sisters and his adorable nieces and nephews. While here in New York, I try to spend as many days as possible with my parents, Josh, and Amy.

I make sure to snag lots of girl time with my sister, especially since I love the updates she gives me on a new possible romance in her life. She's met a guy she likes. News flash: there are all sorts of complications. I mean, she works with him. What could possibly go wrong?

But that's a story for another time.

Meanwhile, I do my best to relax. To let go of my relentless need to plan everything in my life. Babies, after all, have a way of upending plans in the best way possible.

Then, near the end of the summer, I pop.

And I revise the earlier statement I made on Christmas, once our little girl is born.

She's truly the best gift ever.

In the delivery room, Vaughn gazes at our baby with so much love in his eyes, holding her then kissing me. "Now," he says, "*this* is a special delivery."

And four and a half months later, she's with us on Christmas morning, making this holiday even better than the one before.


THE END


**If you missed the other books in the Boyfriend Material series, you can find them here!**
**FREE in KU!**
Asking For a Friend: Amy & Linc
Sex and Other Shiny Objects: Peyton and Tristan
One Night Stand-In: Lola and Lucas
Overnight Service: Josh & Haven

**You might also enjoy the novella Your French Kisses!**
**Turn the page!**

# YOUR FRENCH KISSES

A BOYFRIEND MATERIAL NOVELLA

# ABOUT

*To do list for my last day of my Paris vacation...*

1. Walk along the river

2. Visit all the chocolate shops in the city

3. Wander along the cobblestoned streets.

Things I don't expect to happen...
    1. Meet a charming Englishman while strolling along the Seine

2. Spend the afternoon with him exploring Paris, and kissing. So many French kisses...

3. Board a plane that night wishing I'd gotten his last name.

Besides, you can't fall for someone in one day, especially when you live a world apart...

# WANT TO HEAR?

Want to be the first to learn of sales, new releases,
preorders and special freebies? Sign up for my VIP
mailing list here!

# 1

## REID

*New York*

You know that saying about kids in candy shops?

They've got nothing on a fella in a lingerie shop.

Forget lollipops and chocolate bars. I'll take teddies and corsets. Not for me though.

For . . .

Who do I want it for?

Who am I kidding? I know how to finish that sentence.

I've known it for three years.

But what are the chances I'll see her again? I've nearly given up. I've been searching, stupidly searching this city for a woman I met once upon a time.

I wander into shops, look in windows, imagining I might see her again.

Someday I'll shuck off that wish for good.

But today?

Today, I still have a smidgeon of hope. After all, I can recall with crystal clarity the way she curled a hand over my shoulder, showed me a display of pink and white lace, and said it was her favorite.

I sigh, wishing I'd done something different that day.

One thing different.

Regret is an awful taste.

To counter it, I've given myself three months to entertain a quest.

To pop into shops.

Jewelry stores. Clothing boutiques. Lingerie shops.

What are the chances I'll see my five-hours-in-Paris woman?

I don't let myself answer that question.

Because the three months are nearly over.

But today I'm still looking. Today, I still have a chance, one offered to me by the store owner who I met thirty minutes ago.

Peyton extends a hand, gesturing to the shop she's lured me into.

"And this is my little slice of New York. Welcome to You Look Pretty Today," she says. I made her acquaintance in a coffee shop with my good friend Lucas, and she encouraged me to stop in here, luring me with promises of a single woman who likes water parks.

What can I say?

I'm easy. I like water parks.

But does the woman I met in Paris like them?

I have no idea.

See, I don't even know her last name.

Another regret.

This woman can't possibly be the one I've been looking for. But my time is running out, so why not turn over this stone? You never know.

I walk inside and gesture to the shelves of under-things. "I see you have some wonderful items for my nan," I joke.

"I can definitely find something for her," Peyton says. "I have customers of all ages. But right now, I want you to meet my store manager." She guides me through a display of bustiers.

"Got a little matchmaker in you?"

Her eyes twinkle. "I might. She says she has a thing for British accents."

"Lucky for me."

"Yes, it's totally her weakness."

For a dangerous second, my heart beats faster.

But I tell it to settle down.

It won't be her.

Instead, I scan the lingerie on the shelves, my mind ever so helpfully assembling an image of a svelte blonde in one. A lithe brunette. A pretty redhead.

Nameless women. Faceless women. Never her.

As I wander past a shelf of satin shorts, the scent of lavender drifts into my nose, reminding me of gardens in Paris.

Another memory best forgotten.

After today, I will banish all of them and kick this pointless quest to the curb.

I snap my gaze away from the pretty items, my eyes

returning to Peyton, who has her hand on the arm of her store manager.

I can't see the other woman's face.

But then she rounds the corner as Peyton says to her, "I have someone I want you to meet."

The store manager steps forward, and I am swept back in time.

Brown hair, brown eyes, a smile for days, and dimples. *Those dimples.* I swear I'm seeing things. Seeing her.

Someone I never thought I'd see again.

Someone I've desperately wanted to see again.

And I made a promise that if I ever did, I'd do everything different.

Her eyes lock with mine, and I see that day flash across her irises too.

"It's you?" I ask. Then it's no longer a question. It's a statement. "It's really you."

## 2

## MARLEY

*Paris*

*Nearly three years ago*

I'm not afraid of many things.

Spicy food? Bring it on.

Horror movies? I can handle them.

Camping, hiking, biking, and pitching a tent? Not a problem.

But heights?

Who invented heights?

Clearly someone who hates me.

Heights are officially the worst.

When my girlfriends declare at Café Roussillon over eggs, potatoes, and croissants that today is *the* day, I shake my head. "Au revoir."

"Marley," Bethany says, with a squeeze of my arm and a peppy grin, "You can do it."

She's Rosie the Riveter, tough and badass, but I'm undeterred.

Heights and I don't get along. "I know I can. I don't want to," I say to my college roomie, who wants nothing more than to shoot up to the top of the Eiffel Tower.

"Are you truly saying you don't want to view all of Paris, drink in the vistas, see the Seine cutting across the city like a ribbon?" Emery asks with a sweep of her arm.

I laugh at the image she paints. "You sound like a travel brochure."

"And travel brochures should be followed," she declares as she takes her last bite of egg.

Bethany sips her café noisette—she's gotten me addicted to them—then says, "Paris is for shedding fears."

"And we did that by ordering escargot the other night," I point out as I set down my fork.

Bethany shrugs. "Fine. That was a little terrifying."

"And seriously, thank you for encouraging me, and you are the best, but I swear I have enjoyed seeing the Eiffel Tower from the ground," I say as we pay the check, then leave some euros on the table for the waiter.

"Merci," I call out as we exit and I walk with my friends to the most famous landmark.

This is our last hurrah trip before the three of us scatter across the United States—Bethany to law school in Texas, Emery to a job in San Francisco, and me to business school, starting next week.

Emery pouts. "They say the line will take about two hours, and then we thought we'd do the Montparnasse Tower too. Knock out all the heights today without you."

I nod approvingly. "I like that idea."

"What will you do?" Emery asks.

"Something on the ground," I say playfully as we walk past a gorgeous stone building with curling ironwork framing the tall windows.

What will I do?

I will wander.

It's the thing I like most.

Walking.

Seeing.

Looking.

"I'm going to meet some fabulous Frenchman," I muse as we enter Champ de Mars, the park at the base of the tower. "Have a tryst in a secret passage somewhere in the city, tucked off on a quiet cobblestoned street; kiss a handsome stranger as Édith Piaf plays; and then have a glass of wine and tell my secrets to the river."

Bethany gives me the evil eye, then looks at Emery. "And why are we going to the top of the Eiffel Tower? I want to go with her and have a secret tryst with a gorgeous Frenchman."

Emery purses her lips, her eyes twinkling. "Dinner's on us tonight if you do have that rendezvous. Because you will be entertaining your besties with details."

I stare at the tower, as if deeply considering the offer. "Let me get this straight. If I have a secret tryst, I get one, a tryst; two, a free meal; and three, the memory of the tryst? Sounds like I'll win."

Emery narrows her eyes and stomps her foot. "She bamboozled us. I want what she's having."

"Maybe you'll have a secret love affair at the top of the tower," I say, then hug my best friends goodbye, telling them I'll meet them later, since we need to get ready to leave for an insanely early flight.

I stroll along Rue Saint-Dominique, stopping along the way to check out displays in jewelry stores and clothing boutiques, before I pop into a chocolatier.

A red-haired man behind the counter nods, smiles, and says, "Bonjour."

"Bonjour," I reply, then I ogle the displays of mouth-watering sweets, choose a few, and leave with chocolate in hand.

I cross the boulevard and find a bench by the river. "It's just you and me, river," I say to the water.

I grab a truffle and bite into it. As decadent caramel spreads on my tongue, a man I didn't notice at the end of the bench turns and smiles.

"Good morning."

# 3

## REID

My team came in third, but I can't complain because we didn't even think we'd place.

Tenth was more like our goal.

Hell, *not* finishing in last place would have been an achievement for the Road Flyers, my amateur bike team that competed in a four-day race ending in the City of Lights. It surprised the hell out of the four of us when we landed a spot on the podium.

Tour de France contenders we are not, but it was a right adrenaline rush. Now I'm enjoying a few hours in Paris before I catch a flight back to London, my teammates having taken off already. I'm booked on a different flight.

I pop a chocolate square in my mouth, savoring the orange zest flavor in the dark chocolate, when a brunette with a spray of freckles across her cheeks takes the spot at the end of the bench.

She gazes at the river with a happy sigh, then says, "It's just you and me, river."

My brain is a pinball machine, lighting up, buzzers whirring.

I barely speak a word of French, and she has an American accent. Perhaps it's my lucky day.

"Good morning," I say.

She jerks her gaze to me, then smiles. "Good morning to you too." Her eyes drift to the bag from the shop. "A kindred spirit, I see."

"Well, you know what they say." I gesture to the chocolate like there's some well-known saying about it.

She arches one brow, and it's wildly adorable the way it rises, matching the corner of her lips quirking up. "I don't know what *they* say. What do *they* say?"

I lower my voice, cup my mouth, and stage-whisper, "They say it's never too early to eat chocolate."

"Ah, yes. I have heard that," she says with a nod, dipping her hand into the bag. "I believe it's called chocolate o'clock."

"That's the time my watch is set to as well."

"I have truffles. Want one?" She waggles the bag, and I adopt a new truism immediately. *When a pretty woman offers you chocolate, you say yes.*

"I would love one. As long as you promise they aren't poisoned."

Her expression is intense, overly serious. "As an avid and well-known poisoner, you have my solemn vow," she says, then offers one.

"Well, since it's a solemn vow . . ." I slide closer to her on the bench just as she slides closer to me. I snag a chocolate. "I'm going to trust it's not laced with arsenic."

She scoffs. "Please. I'm all about cyanide. It's stronger and faster."

I stop, chocolate midair. "How do you know that?"

She laughs, a bright, cheery sound. "I read a lot of mysteries. I can tell you the ten deadliest poisons, and the ones most likely to go undetected. But the look on your face is priceless, like you really thought I was going to off you."

I take the chocolate, pop it in, and bite. "I'm living life on the edge. Taking my chances."

"Go you."

When I finish, I hold up my bag of treats. "Want one of my deadly sweets? I made sure to pick up the botulinum-laced variety," I say in a macabre voice.

Her eyes twinkle. "Best morning ever. This is like Russian roulette with chocolate." She chooses a square, then moans around the chocolate. "Oh, that is divine."

*So are your lips.*

*So are your sounds.*

"Glad you like it," I say, as a horn honks. I glance at the river where a boat bleats as it winds its way along the Seine. One of those three-hour cruises perhaps, and something I'd considered for my last day in Paris.

But as much as I enjoy the view of the river and the idea of a day on the water, I like the view on the bench so much more.

And the chance that may be next to me.

I didn't think I'd place in the bike race.

But I went all out.

No reason to do anything differently with the chocolate poisoner. The gorgeous brunette looks to be in her early twenties, only a few years younger than I am. Maybe she's as single as I am too. "I'm Reid. I'm from London. I was in Paris for a bike race with my team. We placed third. I'm heading home tonight."

Her smile is magnetic. "I'm Marley. I'm here with friends before I return to New York to start business school."

I extend a hand and shake hers. "Pleasure to meet you, Marley."

"And you too, Reid," she says, holding my hand longer than I expect as she studies my face. Then she takes a breath, like she's preparing to say something.

And I hope it's not that she needs to leave.

But I don't want to miss a chance to enjoy my last few hours here to the fullest, so I speak first. "There's a new shop a mile away. Fancy a chocolate tour?"

# 4

## MARLEY

It's like he can read my mind. "I was going to ask you the same thing."

One eyebrow quirks. "If I wanted to go on a chocolate tour?"

I wave my hand in the direction of a bookstore I've heard about. "Well, actually to a bookstore. But chocolate works too."

He strokes his chin, like a detective noodling on a case. "Were you going to share all your favorite mysteries featuring death by poisoning?"

I grin mischievously. "I was indeed."

His expression shifts as a delighted grin lights up his handsome face, highlighting his square jaw and his soulful brown eyes. "Chocolate always works, but so do books."

He rises.

I dust off my hands, grab my bag, and tuck the chocolate into my purse. I eye his chocolate bag. "Want me to carry your chocolate?"

He clutches it, pretending to squire it away from me. "A poisoner and a chocolate thief? I've been warned about your type." He wags a finger at me.

"And yet you're walking along the Seine with me," I tease as we stroll.

"True. Apparently, I am easily enchanted by American accents," he says with a wry smile as we wind past a street lamp, and he hands me his bag of chocolate. I tuck it into my purse.

"Your British one isn't too shabby," I say, and then I dive right into questions. Because I can. Because clearly this is a day that is bursting with possibilities and none of those options require holding back. I can't help but think Bethany and Emery will be so jealous, but I'm not doing this to make them jealous. I'm doing this because it feels like what a last day in Paris should be like—a walk beside a river with a handsome stranger, full of potential and flirtation. "You're from London and heading home tonight?"

He nods as we reach the corner of the street, and I let my eyes roam over him. Jeans and a gray T-shirt. He looks about twenty-four or twenty-five. "My bags are packed, and I'm ready to go," he says, and there's the slightest hint of sadness in his voice.

Funny, I feel a touch of it too already. A touch of missing. That's so odd because I've spent only a few minutes with him.

But already we click.

Instantly. Incredibly.

And that's why *not* spending another hour with him in this city would be a missed opportunity.

"Mine too," I say, choosing to enjoy this time fully.

"Are you headed home today?"

"Tomorrow morning. At the crack of dawn," I say with a frown. "Why do six a.m. flights even exist? We have to be at Charles de Gaulle at four thirty."

He shakes his head. "They should be abolished. When I'm in charge of all things, I will outlaw flights at ungodly hours."

"Thank you," I say, like I'm imploring his graciousness. "You have my vote for prime minister."

His brown eyes seem to twinkle. "I thank you for your support." He takes a beat as we cross the avenue. "Have you enjoyed your trip so far, Marley? Summer in Paris can be lovely or vicious."

"It's been lovely. We went to Italy and to Spain and to Paris."

"Quite the jaunt."

"I know, and I'm so lucky we were able to pull this off. My friends are at the top of the Eiffel Tower now, but I didn't want to do that. I happen to detest heights."

"You do?"

I nod, like I'm confessing. "They make me nervous. Like, I can see all the ways they can go wrong. I picture flinging myself down from the top story, and well, that kind of ruins them."

"That would definitely do it."

"Are you afraid of anything? Like, anything totally irrational?"

"Just your standard fear of poisoning by chocolate. But that's hardly irrational," he says with a wink. "Tell me more about your trip."

I picture the last few weeks, recalling our adventures in Rome, our meanderings across the city of Barcelona, and our time in Paris these last few days. "We did it on a shoestring budget," I explain. "We'd made a vow to take a European trip when we graduated, especially since we're all heading in different directions. One of my friends is going to law school. The other starts her first job."

"And you're going to business school?"

"Yes. And while I'm there, I hope to figure out what exactly I want to do in business someday."

"Ah, work. Yes, I've heard of that. It's so dreadful when it gets in the way of bike races and chocolate shops. Shall I ask if you've given any thought yet to what you want to do, or is that a topic best avoided?"

I shrug, but it's the happy kind, because it doesn't entirely bother me that I don't know. "Is it crazy to say I'm not sure? I do want to run my own business. But I'm torn. Sometimes I think I might want to work in public relations and open my own firm. And other times I think I want to market new fashion lines. But I also really like just talking to people, so maybe I should open a cute little boutique, and then it'll turn into a whole line of cute little boutiques. Or I could start a coffee and chocolate shop," I say, tossing out that last option.

"Do you like coffee?"

I adopt a serious stare. "Like it's a religion."

"I pray at that altar too. So, I say you should open a café that sells clothes and then do your own PR for it."

I snap my fingers like I have all the answers now. "There you go. Now I know what I want to do."

"See? It was serendipity that we met," he says playfully as we weave past a Frenchwoman pushing a trolley full of groceries, a baguette poking out the top of one bag.

"But I'll miss Paris," I say, glancing at the bread, then at this man by my side who doesn't feel like a stranger at all. Nor does he feel like the handsome guy I just happened to bump into. He feels like a guy whose path I was meant to cross.

We slow our pace at a light. "I'll miss Paris too," he says as he holds my gaze longer than I expect.

I should look away. I should break the moment. But I don't. Because my stomach flips. And tingles spread down my arms. Then I whisper, "I'm glad I'm afraid of heights."

The light changes, and we cross.

He glances at me out of the corner of his eye, then smiles. His smile is fantastic. So warm and inviting. "I'm glad you're afraid of heights too."

# 5

## REID

I wouldn't say we gorge ourselves on chocolate, but we come damn close.

Marley is a fiend when it comes to sweets, with a sweet tooth that matches mine. I tell her as much as we regard the carnage of our chocolate fiesta on the table —those little wrapper things that hold the chocolates are completely empty. "We have officially made this morning chocolate o'clock every damn second."

"We have," she says, straightening her shoulders like she's issuing a declaration. "And I regret nothing."

"I regret nothing either."

She sets her chin in her hand and meets my eyes. "So, Reid. What do you do in London when you aren't devouring chocolate?"

I lean back in the chair, diving into the quick details. "I'm a designer. I studied graphic design at university. I'm working my way up now, but someday I'd like to have my own company."

She smiles. "I love that. Love that you know what you want to do. What is that like—to know?"

I ponder her question for a few seconds, maybe more. "It's like . . . normal. If that makes sense? I think I've always known. I've loved drawing and designing, and it was always my path. I like this path. I'm glad I'm on it."

"What can you draw?" There's a curious glint in her eyes.

"I happen to be a fantastic doodler. But I'm also tops at drawing caricatures of American girls in chocolate shops."

A laugh seems to burst from her. "Are you serious?"

"As serious as a heart attack." I head to the counter, ask the shopkeeper for a pen and napkin, and return to her, doing a quick rudimentary sketch of her face. It's great fun, because it gives me free rein to stare at her the whole time, to study the shape of her cheekbones, her big brown eyes, the freckles dotting the bridge of her nose.

She sports a grin the entire time, like she's delighting in this moment. I certainly am—it's an unexpected morning in this city with her, and I don't want it to end.

When I'm finished, I show her the napkin.

She chuckles. "That's adorable."

I preen in an over-the-top fashion. "I am known in many parts of the world as an adorable doodler." Then a spate of nerves crawls up my spine. Do I ask her if she wants to keep this? Is that too much for whatever this brief encounter is? This random date that's careening toward its inevitable end in hours?

She speaks first. "I'd like to keep it. May I?"

My chest warms. "It's all yours, Marley."

Neither one of us says anything for a moment. We simply look at each other. Sparks race over my skin, across my chest. This thing, this chemistry, it can't go anywhere. But right now, it feels like we're somewhere special.

And I don't want today to end until it must. I only have a few hours, but I want to spend them with her. "Do you believe in happiness?" I ask.

She tilts her head. "Of course. Why wouldn't I?"

"Do you believe it's possible though? Is it worth chasing?"

"Often I think it's the only thing worth chasing," she says, then adds with a sigh, "but sometimes responsibilities get in the way."

"They do. So you seize your chances for happiness."

"Are you happy?"

I smile. "I'm pretty sure the way I feel right now is the very definition of the word."

The look on her face is magical, like I've said the one perfect thing, so I do my best to keep up my winning streak. "Do you want to go to a bookstore?"

I'm rewarded with another smile. "I would love to. That's the other definition of happiness."

## 6

## MARLEY

The bookstore is quiet, and the delicious smell of pages drifts through the shelves. Patrons lounge in well-worn leather chairs, reading books of poetry or tales of love gone awry.

Truth be told, I have no idea what they're reading, but it feels like that's what they must be inhaling. Or maybe they're devouring stories of strangers who meet for a moment in time, who connect in an instant electric burst, then the firecracker fizzles out, leaving the night pitch-black.

For a second, a storm cloud descends on me.

That's what today is with Reid. I knew that when we first rose from the bench and wandered along the river.

We're a moment in time. A starburst. A spark against the sky that burns bright and fast.

But I'm embracing it.

Even though there's a part of me that's wishing, wanting for today to last beyond this date on the calendar.

Only that's silly.

Today is what it is.

*A day.*

Heck, it's a few hours. A moment in time.

And time should be cherished.

We walk past a table that holds gift books, including a coffee table one with photos of Paris. I run my thumb across the cover then open it, flipping through the images. I point to the ones I like best. Paris in the rain. Paris in the snow. Paris in the sun. "This makes me happy too. These pictures."

He flips to an image of a café. "And that does the trick for me."

I set down the book, and we wander through the mysteries, whispering about poisons and butlers and deadly nights. The steps creak as we head up the staircase to the second floor. It all feels so European. On the second floor, we wander through the stacks of English-language titles.

He picks up a book with a sad-looking man on the cover, staring forlornly into the distance. "He's having a bad day, isn't he?" Reid whispers.

"A terrible one, but if you get that book, yours will become worse."

"I'll return it straight away," he says, tucking it back on the shelf, then stepping closer to me. "Perhaps I should find a book that will only make the day better." He takes a beat. "But that would seem impossible."

I look down, then at him, and smile. My stomach flips when he holds my gaze. "I agree." I lick my lips, then continue along the aisle, where I grab a book with an image of a skillet on the front. "*Top Skillet Recipes to Change Your Life.*" I tap it. "This will make your day amazing."

He nods seriously. "That's true. That does look like a day-brightening book."

"It's your typical airplane read," I tease as we walk past an alcove with an old typewriter perched on a tiny oval table. A handwritten note on the typewriter's keys says *Drink each day.*

I stare at it for a long time. Reid does the same. "Is that a directive to grab a pint?"

"I don't think so," I say pensively.

He gives me an inquisitive look. "What do you think it means, Marley?"

"I think it means drink each day down like it's delicious."

His brow furrows like he's considering this. "That's what you take away from it?"

"I do," I say, feeling certain. "Drink, savor, indulge."

His brown eyes darken as I say those words. "Those are some delicious verbs."

"See? That's what I mean. When you read it that way, it changes the meaning. It's not the best recipes for skillets that will change your life. It's *savoring.* Like the day is a glass of your favorite wine," I say, lifting an imaginary glass. "And you enjoy every last sip."

He's quiet as he seems to study my face, then he sets a hand on my back as we make our way to an open window, stopping to stare at the cobblestoned streets below.

I'm keenly aware that he hasn't removed his hand

from my back. Just the slightest touch without being too much, too presumptuous.

But I wouldn't mind a little presumption.

"Do you enjoy your days like that? Like the note urges?" he asks.

"It's hard to say. I've just finished college, and that's not entirely the place where you can or should drink each day. But I think that's why I've enjoyed this trip so much. I've tried to set aside all the unknowns of what will happen in business school. What I'll decide to do. I'm trying to just enjoy every moment, then learn what I love so I can decide what type of business I do want to run someday. What about you? Do you savor the days?" I ask.

"I don't know if I always do. Sometimes I worry too much about work. The future. What I'm going to do next. The next step. The next job."

"I worry about that too. But I try to tell myself there will be time for that."

"I should take a page from your book and do that too," he says, bumping my shoulder. "Like what I did there?"

I groan, smiling though, because I like contact with him. "I like it a lot."

As he stares out the window, his gaze seems to land on a lanky Frenchman trundling by on a bike. The cyclist holds a bouquet of red balloons.

I laugh, tickled by the image. "He's enjoying his day."

"He's drinking it down." Reid takes his hand from me, and I instantly miss it, wanting it back.

But instead, he reaches for my hand, threading his fingers through mine. His touch lights me up like sparklers on New Year's Eve. "That's better."

Tingles spread across my body. "Are you drinking the day?"

He smiles, and it's both naughty and happy. "This is a day I want to enjoy every last drop of."

"Me too."

We head downstairs, and he grabs a book. The photos of Paris. He buys it, then gives it to me. "This makes me happy. Keep it."

I know I will keep it always. Someday when I'm seventy, I'll look at it and remember the afternoon I spent in Paris with the man from London who made my heart beat faster and harder than it had before.

## REID

The clock is ticking.

That can't be avoided, but I can't let it dictate my every thought.

This is exactly what it is.

A dessert, a drink, a treat.

You don't get to have chocolate for every meal. But you damn well better delight in it when you do.

With her hand in mine, we cross the bridge over the river, passing tourists snapping selfies. We could take a picture. We could exchange numbers. Share the image. But then what?

Trade little texts while she's in New York going to school and I'm an ocean away?

Instead, I squeeze her hand and I focus on the here and now. Only that. Taking mental snapshots. Making memories I can call up. Something I do little of in my digital life. But I want to live fully in this incredible, real moment. "This is the most perfect day. I just want you to know that."

She smiles at me, and it makes my heart flip.

That's unexpected.

Frankly, a little inconvenient too.

Because that'll make it harder to get on the plane. And I have to get on the plane.

"I know that," she says in a bit of a whisper.

"And do you know what would make it even better?" I ask, continuing down this carpe diem path because it's all I can do here.

"Is there anything that could truly make it better?" she asks, a little tease in her tone.

The sound of her voice, a little naughty, a little flirty, winds through me. "Well, there *are* a few things."

Her eyes dance with dirty thoughts. "I can think of a few things too."

"More than a few," I add.

"Lots. So many things."

I groan. "You're going to make this day quite hard. But truth be told, I was thinking we should walk around the Luxembourg Gardens."

She lifts her chin, licks her lips, and says, "Take me there."

How can a woman sound innocent and naughty at the same time? But she does. She absolutely does, and I love it madly.

\* \* \*

We wander through all sorts of flowers. I don't know the names. Or the kinds. Maybe they are irises or lilies. Possibly tulips.

Marley seems to know them all, as we walk through rows of flowers, bursting with color, ruby red and bright pink and sun-drenched yellow.

She rattles off the names, but not like we're in botany class. More like "I've always loved irises" or "Tulips are nature's flirts."

"Are you a tulip?" I ask.

She spins around, wiggles her eyebrows. "What do you think?"

It's a loaded question, and I'm pretty sure I know the answer.

I step closer, inches away. The air is charged, buzzing with possibilities. Somewhere beyond the walls of the garden, the city rolls by.

But here, the garden is an escape with a woman I didn't know mere hours ago. A woman I will say goodbye to in another few hours.

A woman who has lips that look so damn kissable.

"Right now," I say, holding her gaze, "I'm not thinking."

I lift my hand and stroke a thumb along her jaw. She gasps, then whispers, "Don't think."

"I'm definitely not thinking one bit," I say as I move closer, my lips so tantalizingly near hers.

"I'm *only* feeling," she whispers.

I thread my fingers in her hair, press my lips to hers, and drink in a kiss.

I savor every last drop.

I indulge.

And I memorize.

Because I don't want to forget this kiss.

This day. This moment.

It feels different from other moments.

She's different from other women.

Soon we'll go our separate ways, but I always want to remember the American woman I met one afternoon in Paris before I had to catch a flight.

That's how I kiss her.

Like I'll never forget the taste of her sweet lips, the softness of her breath, the way she melts into me.

Or maybe I melt into her. Because this kiss goes to my head. My mind is a blur, and my body is humming sweet yet dirty music as I kiss her softly, tenderly.

Then a little bit harder.

She feels so right in my arms that I have to wonder if I believe in love at first sight.

But that's rubbish.

That's not the way of the world.

That's not the way of *my* world.

Only, for a few stolen moments, it feels like it could be.

Like with a handful of afternoons that spill into the next and the next, we could become that.

She slinks her arms around my neck, bringing me closer, her body pressed to mine.

Yes, a few more days of this, and I'd be in love with her for the rest of my life.

That's the problem.

# 8

## MARLEY

I'm not going to claim to be an expert on kissing.

Sure, I've had my fair share of locking lips. But it's not as if I keep a list of kisses, and if I did, the ratings would be "good, but not great."

When Reid kisses me, I know this is great.

I know this is some kind of kiss.

His lips are soft and confident. His touch is both tender and electric. And he smells so damn good. Like soap and pine and man. My senses are throwing a party as this stranger in a strange land lights me up with his lips, his touch, and something else too.

Something intangible. Something wonderful.

Something that I know will be over far too soon.

Is that why this kiss is so incredible?

Because it exists in its own parallel universe, one where I'm staying in Paris, and he's living here, and we're spending the evenings together wandering the passages and cobblestoned streets as rain falls? Of course, it'll rain in Paris in our universe as we kiss at cafés and shops and under street lamps.

And we make plans to meet again tomorrow.

That's what this kiss is.

A kiss for tomorrow.

A kiss that is tinged with wistfulness, with longing, and with a wish for it to be more than one kiss.

A wish for it to last.

But it can't. Because we're both leaving.

I break the kiss, and he looks lust-drunk.

It's so sexy, and I want to put that look on his face again and again.

"Wow," I say.

"Yeah," he says, scrubbing a hand across his jaw.

"That was . . ."

"Incredible?"

I give him a flirty grin, shaking my head. "Nope."

His brow creases. "No? Am I going to need to try harder?"

"I won't object to that, but I was simply going to say I'm pretty sure it was the best kiss in the history of first kisses."

He leans in close again, dusting those lips over my cheek to my ear, then whispering, "I want to keep writing in that history book."

*This man.*

This man and his funny, clever, vulnerable ways.

"I want that too," I say, but because we can't have what we want, he takes my hand and we walk through the gardens toward the exit.

"I hope I'm not being presumptuous, but I'd like to spend the rest of the day with you until I leave."

I lean my shoulder against his. "You can presume away."

As we exit the gardens, he says, "So, Marley. What would you do if you lived here in Paris?"

"Like, for a job?" I ask as we turn onto a block teeming with pretty boutiques.

"Actually, I wanted to know what you'd do with me, but sure, we can start with work."

"Reid," I say, laughing. "Don't be silly."

"Why is that silly?"

I tap my chest. "I'd do you," I say, bold and direct.

He stops in his tracks, blinking, then drags a hand through his hair. His gaze turns hot, and he reaches for me once more, bringing me close. "You are magnificent."

"So are you."

Then he shows me what a second kiss for the record books is. My knees go weak, my skin sizzles, and I record this moment too.

But, like all of today has so far, it ends too soon. We resume our pace. "So, to answer your question, I'd probably do something where I could talk to people. Maybe work in a shop."

"I'd come to your shop every day."

"Stalker much?" I tease.

He scoffs. "Please. You'd be mine if we lived here. I'd come to your shop at the end of the day, and we'd walk to a brasserie, sit down, order a glass of wine, and watch the city go by. All while we were in our own world."

I swoon, my heart shimmying for him. "Are you the most romantic man I've ever met?"

His grin is so delicious. "I better be."

I run my fingers down his shirt. "You are. It's official."

We walk past a stationery shop selling pens and gorgeous writing paper. The thought briefly occurs to me that we could keep in touch, send letters, little notes.

But keeping in touch seems far too dangerous.

Like leaving out a tempting treat you couldn't actually have.

"Anyway, so what would we do after dinner?" I ask playfully as we pass a jewelry store peddling lockets.

"I'd find all the most romantic places in the city to kiss you again. Since you need to fill in a whole history book of entries."

"So I would record those kisses?"

He nods exaggeratedly. "I would fully expect you to. Record, tabulate, rate."

"You want me to rate your kisses? Maybe I already am."

He tugs me into a quiet alley framed by an arch and curling ivy, and seals his mouth to mine, dropping a hot, tempting kiss on my lips before giving me a hot, naughty stare.

"Are you trying to set a record?" I ask, my skin heating up.

"What would the record be exactly? What's the category?"

"The category is winding me up."

"And I trust it's working?" he asks, a devilish quirk on his lips.

"Everything you do is working."

He smiles, but it fades into a sigh as he presses his forehead to mine. "I wish . . ."

A lump rises in my throat. "I wish too."

"I wish I had another night here. I wish my plane wasn't leaving this evening."

"I wish we could slow down time."

"I wish I met you yesterday." He stops. "Is that crazy?"

I shake my head. "No. But I'm glad I met you today. And I'll miss you tonight."

He swallows, exhales. "It would be crazy, right?"

We both know what the other isn't saying, but I say it anyway. "To see each other again?"

"Yes, I want to. But how can we?"

I shake my head. "I don't know how we could without upending everything."

"I know." He sounds as sad as I feel. "I want to see you again, Marley. You have to know if things were different, I'd take you out tonight, and tomorrow, and the next day. I wouldn't think twice about calling you. Or texting you. I wouldn't take days. Or hours. I'd ask you now and I'd see you tomorrow."

My heart thumps harder for him. "I'd say yes, Reid. I'd definitely say yes."

He presses a kiss to my forehead. "But I live in London."

"And I live in New York."

"And we just met," he adds.

"And I don't know what I'm doing with my life when I finish school."

"You might wind up in Alaska."

I laugh, shaking my head. "Doubtful, but you never know. I do have to focus though. Use the opportunity to figure out what I want to do. I have a scholarship. To keep qualifying for it, I need to hit a minimum GPA. That has to be my priority."

"As it should be."

I draw a deep breath, prepping myself to say something hard. "We need to just enjoy this for what it is."

He smiles, one corner of his lips curving up. "One perfect afternoon in Paris?"

"The most perfect one ever recorded."

"Let's keep making it better," he says, and that seems like a fair enough deal to me.

# 9

## REID

There is no doubt.

I can't imagine looking back on my life and ever having had a better day.

In fact, it's so damn good that I'm tempted, more than I've been tempted before, to do something wildly ridiculous.

Like try to stay in touch.

As we walk by the Tuileries, I want to say, *Screw this long-distance issue. Give me your number and let's talk.*

But what would that look like? Late-night phone chats? All-day-long texts that would distract me as I tried to work my way up at the firm and as she went to school?

That's mad.

So we talk now instead. I ask her about her favorite things.

She tells me about her friends, how Bethany is a hugger and Emery is a giggler, and how the three of them were like sisters in school, depending on each other, helping each other through painful breakups and even more painful exams.

When it's my turn, I tell her about my sister and how we've always been close friends. I talk about the books I love, the articles that capture my interest, and my allergy to early mornings. I also confess that pop music is brilliant.

"Pop like Taylor Swift or Katy Perry?" she asks.

"Or P!nk or Lady Gaga."

"Whoa. I like you." She squeezes my arm.

"Thank you. I was hoping I'd pass the pop music test. And that you'd have the same taste in music."

She arches a dubious brow. "Did I say I had the same taste? I'm a Bruce Springsteen gal. Bryan Adams. And the Eagles."

"What generation are you, woman? Lost in time?"

"I like Jackson Browne too."

"Are you secretly fifty? Were you born in the seventies?"

"I'm retro."

"You can call it that, but I've never met anyone with a seventies retro kink."

She wiggles her brows. "Maybe that's not my only kink."

I groan. "That's a door I'm going to kick wide open. What are the others? I require details. Each chapter, and every sordid verse," I say as we pass a boutique with a pink window display showing off teddies and bras, panties and stockings.

"I have a wicked fetish for lingerie," she says, pointing at all the lacy numbers.

"You do?" I ask, my voice gravelly, thick with a new bout of lust.

She stares longingly at a white-and-pink bra with some sort of crisscross straps. "That's my favorite. I never bought a lot of lingerie in college since it's expensive, but I have always loved the prettiest things. I love looking and touching, and I love the way wearing them makes me feel."

I loop an arm around her waist. "How does it make you feel?"

She turns to me and whispers, "Beautiful."

My body longs for her. My mind aches for her. I bring her closer, unable to resist kissing this woman. "You are beautiful," I say, as I kiss her one more time.

A slow and lingering kiss.

If I'm not careful, I'll ditch my flight simply to spend one more night with her.

The thought is tempting. So damn tempting.

And once it lands in my head, the idea that I could do that? It's too powerful to ignore. "I could stay another night," I blurt out.

Her eyes flutter open. "Tonight?"

"Yes. I know it sounds crazy. Insane, even."

"No, it doesn't," she says. "But . . ."

I swallow roughly. "But what?"

"But what if I don't want to get on my plane in the morning?"

"Then you'd stay here with me," I say, even though we both know that's a foolish dream. I won't be here either.

She ropes her arms around my neck. "Fine. I'll stay

here with you, and we'll dance on a rooftop garden, and we'll watch the stars. We'll go to The Marais and duck in and out of antique shops, and pop into the Musée Rodin whenever the mood strikes."

I pick up the thread easily. "There are Monets to be seen. Don't forget the Musée d'Orsay."

"We'll kiss in front of a Van Gogh that's rumored to be magical. And then there will be more magic when we go clubbing in Oberkampf."

I groan appreciatively. "I like your story of our romance. Clubbing in Oberkampf sounds dirty and delicious."

"That's how we'll dance, Reid. Our bodies will be tangled together."

"Inseparable," I add, my voice going low, smoky.

"People will watch us," she says. "They'll pretend not to, but they won't be able to take their eyes off us."

"They'll be jealous of the young lovers," I add, stroking her hair, running a thumb across her jaw, picturing our sultry nights.

"They'll be jealous because they'll know that when we leave, we'll be *that* couple."

"The couple who can't take their hands off each other."

"Or their eyes," she adds.

I can't stand this. I can't take the tension. Or the reality that I'm leaving and so is she. I press a kiss to her lips, then ask the inevitable. "What would happen if we stayed in touch?"

She looks up at me, and her voice comes out trembling. "What do *you* think would happen?"

The look in her eyes. The tremor in her voice. I have to stop pushing and pressing. She's going to graduate school. She has no room for a long-distance lover.

But this stupid organ in my chest is galloping out of control. I try to talk back to it. *For fuck's sake, it's been four hours.*

But what if four hours is enough?

Enough to know?

Enough to feel?

Enough to try to stay in touch with a woman going to business school halfway around the world?

*Exactly.*

I must focus on goals. Hers, and mine. She doesn't need a man distracting her from her studies and scholarships with nightly texts. And I don't have the wherewithal or the means to travel to New York to see her regularly.

I dig down deep, then answer with my brain. "We'd fall for each other and it would mess up our lives. That's why we're going to do something else."

Her brow knits. "What would that be?"

I grab her hand, lead her into a café, order two espressos, and ask her for the book from the store. The Paris photo one.

"You're taking it back," she says with a pout, clutching it.

"I would never do such a horrid thing. I have other plans for it."

She proffers it from her bag and slides it across the table to me.

I ask for a pen, and she hands me that too.

I write inside.

*Someday when I run into you again, because I know I will, we'll have more than one perfect afternoon. We'll have endless time.*

I turn it around and show her.

Her expression shifts. A lone tear streaks down one cheek, then another.

But she seems to collect herself, because she straightens her shoulders and says ever so softly, "I believe in that someday."

## 10

## MARLEY

I look at my watch.

He looks at his.

There is no more time.

But I want to squeeze every last second out of this fantastic afternoon. I walk with him to his hotel, where he hands the porter a few euros and the man brings him his bag from bell check.

Reid turns to me. We stand in the tiny lobby with music playing softly in a romantic language. I can't make out a word, but I know it's a sad song, a story of lovers torn apart.

"Come here," he whispers.

"I'm already here."

"I want to give you my last name. I want to know yours too. But if I do, I worry I'll spend all my time googling you."

"I know that's all I'd do, so we probably shouldn't." I swallow down the stone in my throat. "This is crazy. How is this possible?"

With a smile, he shrugs, then says wistfully, "French kisses?"

I smile back, full of melancholy too. "Your French kisses."

"Our French kisses." He cups the back of my head, then lowers his voice. "You have to know I want to say screw responsibilities. I want to say I'll see you tomorrow. But I'm not going to say that."

I shake my head, my throat tight. "You can't say that. I can't either."

"And you shouldn't. But today is making me believe in something else."

My heart speeds up. "What's that?"

"That if we both believe in happiness, we'll find it. We'll remember this day fondly. And if it's meant to be, we'll find each other again."

I love the thought, but how can that happen? "How? If I try to find you, I won't be able to do the things I need to do."

"Don't try now. Go to grad school. Somehow we'll meet again." He whispers in my ear, "And when I see you again, I won't get on a plane. I'll take you home with me."

I bury my face in the crook of his neck, wondering how I went from being afraid of heights to being afraid of falling in an entirely different way.

I let another tear fall, then I pull back, fasten on a smile, and tell him the full truth. "And when you ask, I'll say yes."

We leave the hotel. He hails a taxi, and it's here far too soon.

Everything is ending far too soon.

But somewhere deep inside, I keep hoping it's only the beginning.

Especially when he gives me one last kiss.

Then we say goodbye.

## 11

***

## REID

*London*

*A month later*

I don't think about Marley.

I don't let my mind wander to the lovely American woman with the freckles.

I refuse to let my thoughts stray to her soulful eyes, her lush hair, her winning smile.

And I do not under any circumstances consider her warm sense of humor, her wryness, the way she teased me coupled with the ways she didn't tease me. My God, the woman was so open, so heartfelt.

I'll never meet someone like her again.

But I don't think about that whatsoever.

If I did, I'd be a sad sack.

And I'm not. At all.

I have work to do, a business to build, and contacts to develop.

And that's why when I go to New York for a project, I don't look her up.

How could I?

I don't know her last name.

Sure, I could search all the Marleys in New York in business school. But there are many business schools in New York, and surely many Marleys. So if I did that, I'd have to punish myself with no more football, no more books, no more chocolate.

I'd have to ask my best mates to take away my man card.

She was a moment in time.

And only that.

And as I once read on the back of a book jacket I designed, "Some relationships were meant to last for a lifetime. Some for a day."

My chest punches.

What a stupid saying.

I should have asked for her name, her number.

I should have done any or all of the above.

Except I won't and I can't.

After a meeting, I walk through the Village, past the NYU business school.

Is that where she went?

No idea.

But just in case, I give myself an hour.

One hour to sit.

To think.

To hope.

It's insane in many ways.

Not to mention completely pathetic.

But I can't seem to stop.

I don't want to stop.

I want to see her. And walk up to her and say, *Let's do that over*.

But when sixty minutes pass and there is no Marley, of course I resign myself to the cold realization that what happened in Paris was meant to be one perfect afternoon.

Nothing more.

And over the next two years as I travel back and forth to New York and make contacts and network with American designers on shared projects, including a fella named Lucas, I force myself to move on from Marley.

I even date.

It's horrid, but so it goes.

# 12

## MARLEY

*New York*

*Two years later*

I survive.

I survive two years of business school.

I make it through the toughest classes of my life.

And I survive missing the man I spent the most magical afternoon with.

For a while, I didn't think I would.

I was certain I'd break down, fly to London, and knock on all the doors of all the design firms.

But I didn't.

We made an agreement.

That we'd rely on fate.

That serendipity would have to bring us back together.

So I didn't look for him, and while I wasn't searching, I found something else in two years of classwork.

Myself.

My goals.

My dreams.

And I might even know what I want to do.

Someday I want a shop that becomes one of many. I plan to open a boutique that women flock to and love, and then I'll open more.

But first I need to start with a basic J-O-B.

I'm offered jobs at banks and accounting firms.

But I turn them down.

Because I can't stop thinking about something I said in Paris.

*I'd probably do something where I could talk to people. Maybe work in a shop.*

I'm still drawn to that.

When I'm offered an entry-level job at a lingerie shop with the potential to move up, I jump on it.

It might not sound like a sexy offer for a business school grad, but it works for me. It's a chance to learn the ropes.

And I'm determined to find my way.

I do that every day for the next year, figuring out how to run a business, understanding what it entails, and helping customers every day.

A woman named Olivia comes to the shop once a month or more, and we chat about travel, life, and lingerie.

"My fiancée has a thing for lingerie," she tells me in a whisper on one of her visits. "But then, so do I."

"Sounds perfect that you both love it," I say, then I show her some of our new styles, and she oohs and ahhs.

As I ring her up, we chat more, and she asks me if I plan on going back to Paris anytime. I sigh, a little wistfully. "I hope so. I'd love too. I spent the most wonderful day there."

She studies my face for a few seconds. "Did you fall for someone in Paris once upon a time?"

I startle, surprised. Am I that easy to read? Maybe I am. "Something like that."

"Then I hope you find your something like that again," she says, and as she turns to leave, she offers a smile and says, "Maybe you'll find him again."

"Maybe I will," I say but I'm not sure I believe that.

So I focus on other matters.

The store, my skills, my work.

I become friendly with my boss, even more so when she falls in love with her best friend, and it's reminiscent of how I felt in Paris. Fine, she's known this guy for ten years and I knew Reid for five hours, but those five hours marked me.

They marked my heart, and I kept them close.

The memories are as sharp as they've ever been.

I'm not a nun. I haven't held out for him, because that would make me foolish. But I haven't met anyone who makes my heart trip like that man did.

Which feels infinitely silly when I let myself break it down like it's a business problem. It seems like math ought to defy the probability of that happening.

But nothing about that day seemed like math.

And it has stayed with me.

Maybe it always will.

* * *

One day as I'm helping Peyton plan the next season's looks, a British man walks into the store. He's older, in his fifties, and he's charming as he buys a nightie for his wife.

"Thank you two lovely ladies so very much," he says when he leaves.

I sigh. "I love British accents," I admit to Peyton.

"You do?"

"I do. I met this guy once in Paris for a day. He was British, and ever since then, I swear I perk up when I hear an Englishman. Like I'm hoping it might be him."

She smiles. "Maybe someday it will be."

I shake my head. "That won't happen."

"You never know . . ." she says, letting her voice trail off. "Where is he?"

"I don't know. I don't even know his last name. I only know where he lives and his profession."

"You could try googling him."

I have tried. I've punched in every permutation of "Reid" and "London" and "design firm." But I've found nothing. I wish I had one more detail. One more clue. Something else to add to the search string. Something that would lead me to him.

But there are none.

That night when I'm home alone, I open the book and read his inscription.

.   .   .

*Someday when I run into you again, because I know I will, we'll have more than one perfect afternoon. We'll have endless time.*

I trace the words.

Then I close the book and send a thank you to the universe that I had that moment.

That's all it'll ever be.

I look at the napkin drawing one more time, hoping I'll find his name. His number. A secret message. But I've turned it over a thousand times, and it's only a drawing.

And a memory of a moment, a small slice of time.

The most wonderful moment I've ever had.

One I miss terribly.

In the morning I wake up with a start, a tingling sensation in the back of my mind. Déjà vu. Like when you see an actor and can't place him until you remember he was the third guy on the left in episode seventeen.

It's there.

One more detail.

*I was in Paris for a bike race with my team. We placed third.*

Reid said that to me.

Will it be enough?

I swallow nervously, grab my computer, and send a wish out to fate.

Anticipation builds in me as I google "bike races in Paris" during the time I was there.

And I find one.

My heart speeds up. It races like a locomotive along the tracks as I scan the names of the teams, then the members.

And I gasp.

Because there it is.

Reid Martin.

My whole body is tense, alive with possibilities.

I drop the name into google, and I gasp in a whole new way.

He's a designer.

*And he lives in New York.*

I spend the morning trying to figure out what I'll say when I email him at work. But I don't plan what to say if he walks into the shop that afternoon.

I am speechless.

## 13

---

## REID

I check out a florist on the Upper East Side.

I pop into a jewelry store in Murray Hill.

I stop by a lingerie shop in the Village.

It's getting to be a habit with me.

But it's one I can't break.

I haven't broken it since Lucas asked me to set up shop with him in New York a few months ago. We'd already been working together on a number of projects, and most of our clients were in the city. It only made sense to pack up my bags and follow the business.

That's what I'd been building toward for the last few years in London.

I didn't move here to find her.

I moved here for business.

Yet looking for her has become a hobby.

Perhaps I am a stalker.

Or maybe I'm just a guy who can't quite give up.

I give myself a deadline.

I tell myself that I'll allow myself three months of

checking out shops, of looking for her in person, since I've had no luck finding her through online searches. I simply don't have enough details.

Instead, I check out places she might work.

I'm like a detective chasing down clues.

But I'm reaching the end of the line.

Until the day some of my business partner's old friends show up at a coffee shop and tell me I must come along to a lingerie store.

What are the chances it'll be hers?

But it's my last chance, so I take it.

And then I see the face I've been dreaming of.

## 14

---

## MARLEY

I'm seeing things.

There is no other explanation.

There is no other reason.

I can't possibly be looking at Reid.

Reid Martin, who I've been composing an email to in my head all morning.

He looks just as handsome as he did that day, if not more so.

"It's you," he says in a whisper laced with disbelief.

"It's you," I say, trembling, unsure too.

Because when your wildest dreams come true, you still don't believe them.

After all, he could be married. He could be involved. He could have thought we were foolish.

"How are you?" he asks, the most pedestrian of questions, as he walks over to me, wonder in his eyes.

"I'm great," I say in a voice that hardly feels like my own. It's like I'm talking from within a dream. "And you?"

"I've never been better. Literally."

"You look . . ." My voice trails off. It's choked with emotion. I don't want to let on that I've dreamed of this magical moment. But I can't fake it.

"You look real. You look like all I've wanted," he says, taking the leap first.

It unlocks my heart. It unlocks everything I've stored up since I met him and we spent the most magical day together. "I missed you."

"And I made a promise in Paris."

"What was that?" I ask, my voice pitching up.

"That if I found you again, I'd make sure we spent a lot more than five hours together."

I beam. Like the sun is shining inside me. I look at my watch. "What do you know? I have no place to be and nothing but time."

His smile matches mine as he takes my hands. "Have dinner with me tonight. And tomorrow. And the next day."

## 15

## REID

*That night*

That part about feeling like a kid in a sweet shop?

That's nothing compared to a man waiting for a date with the woman he can't get out of his head.

I never believed in *the one who got away* till I met her.

Till I *let* her get away.

I had my reasons at the time.

They made sense in my head.

And I knew, too, in my heart that we weren't a possibility. There was too much between us then.

Now?

I'm determined to make sure the woman I've been searching for doesn't slip through my fingers.

As I wait at the restaurant, I adjust my tie, then smooth my hands down the front of my trousers. I grab my whiskey and knock back a thirsty gulp, then I look at the time again.

*Time.*

The thing that mocked me three years ago.

Now, my life is different.

The question is . . . will hers be?

The door opens.

I turn around. My heart skips all its beats.

She walks in, looking as innocent and as seductive as she did three years ago along the River Seine.

Those freckles.

Her eyes.

Her curves.

And what's that?

A hint of a pink bra strap.

I groan.

She walks over to me. "Good evening."

I say nothing.

I made a promise to myself that if I had the good fortune to see her again, I'd do something else first.

Something that made me lose my mind for her.

I stand, sweep a hand through her hair, and tug her close for a kiss.

It's like going back in time.

It's as fantastic as I remembered.

She's soft and warm, and she kisses back with a hunger I didn't forget. I didn't inflate. I didn't exaggerate.

This woman kisses me like we're kismet.

Like we're serendipity.

Like we simply met at the wrong moment in time,

but fate was on our side, guiding us back to the right moment.

Because now is right.

When we break the kiss, she smiles like she has a naughty secret. "It's a fact— best first kiss ever."

"Was that our first?" I ask with a grin that I can't erase.

"It's the first of many more to come," she declares.

*This woman.*

I'm not letting her go.

I take her hand, guide her to the table I reserved, then tell her, "Just so you know, I'm not letting you get away this time."

She squeezes back. "Just so you know, I'm not going anywhere."

"I have one question though," I say.

"Go for it."

"Do you like water parks?"

"I love them."

"Excellent."

We have dinner and we catch up, and it's as magical as it was that day nearly three years ago.

But more so.

Because it's not winding up.

It's unfurling into the future.

That's where I go with her that night when she invites me to her place. Well, I go other places too. I take her to the heavens and back, and she calls out my name countless times, and I say hers too as she digs her nails into my back.

But it's all the future.

She's my future.

In the morning we exchange numbers, and I send her the first text from beside her in bed.

**Reid:** Just so you know, I'm falling in love with you.

**Marley:** Just so you know, I've been falling in love with you for three years.

The time is finally right. It's finally ours. And with a little bit of searching, and a whole lot of fate, we have what I wrote in the book that day in Paris.

Endless time.

\* \* \*

**Want more in this world? Be sure to try my brand new crossover standalone romance, My So-Called Sex-Life! It's FREE IN KU!**

# BE A LOVELY

Want to be the first to know of sales, new releases, special deals and giveaways? Sign up for my newsletter today!

Want to be part of a fun, feel-good place to talk about books and romance, and get sneak peeks of covers and advance copies of my books? Be a Lovely!

# MORE BOOKS BY LAUREN

I've written more than 100 books! **All of these titles below
are FREE in Kindle Unlimited!**

**Double Pucked**

A sexy, outrageous MFM hockey romantic comedy!

**Puck Yes**

A fake marriage, spicy MFM hockey rom com!

**The Virgin Society Series**

Meet the Virgin Society – great friends who'd do anything for
each other. Indulge in these forbidden, emotionally-charged,
and wildly sexy age-gap romances!

The RSVP

The Tryst

The Tease

**The Dating Games Series**

A fun, sexy romantic comedy series about friends in the city
and their dating mishaps!

The Virgin Next Door

Two A Day

The Good Guy Challenge

**How To Date Series (New and ongoing)**

Four great friends. Four chances to learn how to date again. Four standalone romantic comedies full of love, sex and meet-cute shenanigans.

My So-Called Sex Life

Plays Well With Others

**A romantic comedy adventure standalone**

**A Real Good Bad Thing**

**Boyfriend Material**

Four fabulous heroines. Four outrageous proposals. Four chances at love in this sexy rom-com series!

Asking For a Friend

Sex and Other Shiny Objects

One Night Stand-In

Overnight Service

**Big Rock Series**

My #1 New York Times Bestselling sexy as sin, irreverent, male-POV romantic comedy!

Big Rock

Mister O

Well Hung

Full Package

Joy Ride

Hard Wood

**Happy Endings Series**

Romance starts with a bang in this series of standalones following a group of friends seeking and avoiding love!

Come Again

Shut Up and Kiss Me

Kismet

My Single-Versary

## Ballers And Babes

Sexy sports romance standalones guaranteed to make you hot!

Most Valuable Playboy

Most Likely to Score

A Wild Card Kiss

## Rules of Love Series

Athlete, virgins and weddings!

The Virgin Rule Book

The Virgin Game Plan

The Virgin Replay

The Virgin Scorecard

## The Extravagant Series

Bodyguards, billionaires and hoteliers in this sexy, high-stakes series of standalones!

One Night Only

One Exquisite Touch

My One-Week Husband

## The Guys Who Got Away Series

Friends in New York City and California fall in love in this fun and hot rom-com series!

Birthday Suit

Dear Sexy Ex-Boyfriend

The What If Guy

Thanks for Last Night

The Dream Guy Next Door

## Always Satisfied Series

A group of friends in New York City find love and laughter in this series of sexy standalones!

Satisfaction Guaranteed

Never Have I Ever

Instant Gratification

PS It's Always Been You

## The Gift Series

An after dark series of standalones! Explore your fantasies!

The Engagement Gift

The Virgin Gift

The Decadent Gift

## The Heartbreakers Series

Three brothers. Three rockers. Three standalone sexy romantic comedies.

Once Upon a Real Good Time

Once Upon a Sure Thing

Once Upon a Wild Fling

## Sinful Men

A high-stakes, high-octane, sexy-as-sin romantic suspense series!

My Sinful Nights

My Sinful Desire

My Sinful Longing

My Sinful Love

My Sinful Temptation

## From Paris With Love

Swoony, sweeping romances set in Paris!

Wanderlust

Part-Time Lover

## One Love Series

A group of friends in New York falls in love one by one in this sexy rom-com series!

The Sexy One

The Hot One

The Knocked Up Plan

Come As You Are

## Lucky In Love Series

A small town romance full of heat and blue collar heroes and sexy heroines!

Best Laid Plans

The Feel Good Factor

Nobody Does It Better

Unzipped

## No Regrets

An angsty, sexy, emotional, new adult trilogy about one young couple fighting to break free of their pasts!

The Start of Us

The Thrill of It

Every Second With You

## The Caught Up in Love Series

A group of friends finds love!

The Pretending Plot

The Dating Proposal

The Second Chance Plan

The Private Rehearsal

## Seductive Nights Series

A high heat series full of danger and spice!

Night After Night

After This Night

One More Night

A Wildly Seductive Night

## Joy Delivered Duet

A high-heat, wickedly sexy series of standalones that will set your sheets on fire!

Nights With Him

Forbidden Nights

**Unbreak My Heart**

A standalone second chance emotional roller coaster of a romance

**The Muse**

A magical realism romance set in Paris

**Good Love Series of sexy rom-coms co-written with Lili Valente!**

**I also write MM romance under the name L. Blakely!**

**Hopelessly Bromantic Duet (MM)**

Roomies to lovers to enemies to fake boyfriends

Hopelessly Bromantic

Here Comes My Man

**Men of Summer Series (MM)**

Two baseball players on the same team fall in love in a forbidden romance spanning five epic years

Scoring With Him

Winning With Him

All In With Him

MM Standalone Novels

A Guy Walks Into My Bar

The Bromance Zone

One Time Only

The Best Men (Co-written with Sarina Bowen)

Winner Takes All Series (MM)

A series of emotionally-charged and irresistibly sexy standalone MM sports romances!

The Boyfriend Comeback

Turn Me On

A Very Filthy Game

Limited Edition Husband

Manhandled

If you want a personalized recommendation, email me at laurenblakelybooks@gmail.com!

# CONTACT

I love hearing from readers! You can find me on TikTok at LaurenBlakelyBooks, Instagram at LaurenBlakelyBooks, Facebook at LaurenBlakelyBooks, or online at LaurenBlakely.com. You can also email me at laurenblakelybooks@gmail.com